EDEN

"Breathtaking – one of the finest pieces of YA writing I've ever come across." *Anthony McGowan*

"Lyrical, evocative, tense and utterly un-putdownable, *Eden* is a modern day *Rebecca*. One of the best books I have read in years." *Catherine Bruton*

"I devoured *Eden* in hungry gulps, unable to put it down, just the way I read as a teenager! It's thrilling, compulsive, beautifully written and powerful in its evocation of a person, and a place… A gripping story that will haunt the reader for a long time after the last page is turned." *Julia Green*

"Heart-stopping, unsettling and utterly beautiful." *Liz Bankes*

Also by Joanna Nadin:

WONDERLAND

"The lure of danger will hook readers, and the story's shocking revelations will make them go back to realize what they missed." *Booklist*

"Teens harbouring a secret wish to be anyone other than who they are will identify with Jude's struggle." *Kirkus Reviews*

UNDERTOW

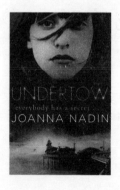

"Billie Paradise is looking for a place to belong, and finds herself tangled up with the ghosts of the past... Beautifully written, emotionally powerful, a novel you won't forget." *Cathy Cassidy*

"A powerful and emotional read." *Bliss magazine*

"A quiet and emotional mystery, this thoughtful novel will suit smart and sensitive readers." *School Library Journal*

"This is a stirring, elegant, and winning effort for Nadin." *Booklist*

"A very eloquently told tale of a family filled with deceitful secrets that have ruined many lives [... *Undertow*] will appeal to a general young adult and adult audience looking for a great read." *VOYA*

EDEN

JOANNA NADIN

WALKER
BOOKS

First published in Great Britain 2014 by Walker Books Ltd
87 Vauxhall Walk, London SE11 5HJ

2 4 6 8 10 9 7 5 3 1

Text © 2014 Joanna Nadin
Front cover photographs © 2014 Shutterstock; Ralf Schultheiss / Getty Images;
Rubberball / Mike Kemp / Getty Images

The right of Joanna Nadin to be identified as author of this
work has been asserted by her in accordance with the
Copyright, Designs and Patents Act 1988

This book has been typeset in Fairfield

Printed and bound in Great Britain by Clays Ltd, St Ives plc

British Library Cataloguing in Publication Data:
a catalogue record for this book is
available from the British Library

ISBN 978-1-4063-4699-2

www.walker.co.uk

For the wallflowers

NOW

I STILL dream of Eden. Not the burnt, broken shell it is now, nor even the sweating, stifling coffin it became that last summer, when it was shrouded in dust sheets, awaiting burial like a corpse. No, the Eden in my mind is the one from my childhood when my entire world was contained within its cool, granite walls and high hedges, and my imagination played out on its velvet lawns and in the creeping dampness of the woods.

The slightest, strangest thing will open up a chink in my veneer: the curve in a flock-papered wall; the plastic taint of squash from a child's beaker; a nettle sting on a grazed knee. And then through this crack the memories swarm, teeming from unfathomed depths into my consciousness, like the swift surge of ants across a careless drip of jam. I remember the faded roses on the drawing room carpet under my always-bare feet, and the bright rhomboids of light from the leaded windows that cast their own tessellation on the black and white check of the hallway tiles. I remember the sound of Bea's breath, the comfort of its steady rise and fall as she lay in the narrow wooden bed next to mine.

Then these clear-as-yesterday sensations are joined by other fleeting glimpses in time, thirteen-year-old Bea reading, stretched across a princess bed in a turret, locked away from our world and immersed in another, or sixteen-year-old Bea holding court in the back room of a smoky pub, its carpet sticky with spilt lager and Coke and patterned with the fallen ash from her cigarettes, or almost-adult Bea's laughter spilling out through the trees like bright butterflies as sweet-sixteen-year-old me runs down the path to the boathouse to meet her. An unceasing parade of Kodak moments surround me – a swirling dustbowl of memory that lifts me up and sends me soaring. Like Icarus seeking the sun, I fly so high that the trees become the odd, spongy miniatures from a toy train set, the house a shrunken version of itself rendered in painted plastic, and the creek a sliver of foil stuck down with a brush and glue.

Then I see them: Bea and a boy, my boy – Tom – or one I want for my own. Their brown-limbed bodies are close, too close. Their fingers are touching, now, their lips. A hot hand rests on a sand-spackled back. I hear a sound, his, of pleasure; then my own, of disgust. Bea could have had anyone. So why him? Why Tom?

And I begin to fall – a giddy, stomach-swirling tumble down towards the water. It is a fall I cannot possibly survive. I hit the surface, and my breath is knocked from my body, but I don't sink. Instead I'm thrown, gasping, onto the shore of the "now" me: the writer, her fingers poised mid-sentence above a keyboard; the mother kneeling at the refrigerator door, milk carton in hand; the wife wrapped around the familiar curve of her husband's spine in a bedroom twenty-something years and two hundred and more miles away from Eden.

I wait for my heart to slow and my breathing to even out into a tick-tock rhythm, like a clock counting out a life in hours and minutes. And then I begin the game. Not an I-spy or a who-am-I or any of the charades that Bea and I would conjure up and convolute to fill a rainy afternoon or dark winter morning, but a darker game, filled with the danger and deliciousness of truth or dare. It is a game of "what ifs" and "if onlys". If I could turn back time; if I could have been different – looked different; if I had said this and not said that. Would there have been a different ending? Would Eden still stand? Would Bea still be alive?

But the game is pointless. For I can't change what has been. Only what I take from it. Besides, paradise is not lost in a single day. Eden didn't fall in the furnace of that afternoon, nor because of the match struck a year before by a single kiss. A kiss that at the time meant everything, meant the world – or at least the end of mine – but which I know now was worth less than nothing. The truth is that the decay had crept in to Eden long ago. Only I, rose-tinted, and blinded by hope, didn't see the flames already crackling beneath my feet. The tinder set for every loss, every argument between me and Bea, every "wish you weren't here"; kindling stacked on high over months and years, until Eden's very foundations were a dessicated, precarious heap, waiting for a single Lucifer to be dropped.

JULY 1988

"EVANGELINE?"

The sound of my name wrenches me from the paradise inside my head – the moss-ridden lawn between my toes, the clink of glasses of cream soda, their ice-cream hats melting in the summer heat. I am back to the cold, hard corners of the classroom, and the whispers of twenty pinafore-clad girls with polished accents and shinier hair.

"Sir?"

I wait for Mr Winters to repeat his demand for Pythagoras' theorem or Occam's razor or a verse of "Kubla Khan". But then I see he's not alone. At his side is Miss Crane, the school secretary, a pinched woman in glasses with the perpetual scent of breath mints and witch hazel. My stomach lurches with fear and possibility, because I'm not being summoned to give an answer, but to see the headmistress.

I stand quickly and my chair clatters to the ground. As I stoop to right it, I feel the pink heat of embarrassment bloom across my cheeks and the prick of salt in the corners of my eyes. I bite my lip – a trick Bea taught me as a way to stop the tears coming – but I bite too hard and, as I walk past the stares and the sniggers, I taste the metallic tang of blood.

The headmistress, Mrs Buttle, is a hard-faced woman with a tight, grey perm and lips like leather, and her office is the setting for only two scenes: punishment or devastation. But I can see by the depth and direction of creases in her high brow that it is pity, not anger that furrows it now.

"Sit down, Evie." Her voice is low, grave, and coloured with the tone of a command, not a question, so I do as I am told.

Silence hangs heavy, like the drape of the velvet curtains, but my head – fuelled by a diet of too many novels and an unhealthy interest in the news – buzzes with possibilities: maybe Uncle John has had a heart attack. Not a fatal one, but one that means he will have to return to Eden and be nursed by his devoted-again wife. Or perhaps it is Aunt Julia who is sick. Perhaps she has cancer – not so bad that she will die – but just bad enough that he cannot leave her. He will realize he still loves her, and call off the divorce and the house sale.

But this isn't about Uncle John, or Aunt Julia.

"It's Beatrice," Miss Buttle says. Then, as if I may be confused or slow-witted she adds: "Your cousin?"

I feel my chest contract, my throat tighten. I clutch at straws: maybe she's been cast in a film and had to leave uni after just a year. Or she's been offered a part on Broadway. Yes, that's it. And she's asked me to go with her. I will finally escape from this school on a hill with its Dettol- and deodorant-reeking dorms and peeling paint to a world where the streets are, if not paved with gold, then at least lit with pink neon. Our anger and our disappointment in each other is gone and we've remembered who we love best and who we need more than anyone. We'll go to America, and then back to Eden, to those endless summers of before, where the wide world was the creek and centre stage was just the two of us.

But I'm wrong. Bea is going nowhere.

"There's been an accident; I'm so sorry. Bea … Bea is dead."

And in a single sentence my world falls apart.

The words come in waves, a strange hollow ring to them as if spoken into a glass then tipped over me, soaking me, penetrating my clothes, my skin, my soul.

"There was a fire," she says. "At her hall."

"House," I hear myself correct. "She lives in a house now." Then another correction, unspoken this time: "lived". I close my eyes and wish for the sudden jolt and flood of relief that comes with waking from a bad dream. But there's none. When I open my eyes again, I'm still in the headmistress's office with the smell of custard creams on a tea plate turning my stomach. And my cousin is still dead.

"She was asleep, they think. So she wouldn't have felt anything."

I taste the bitterness of bile at the back of my mouth and have to suppress the sudden urge to vomit. This is a lie. And I'm transported. I'm no longer caught in the claustrophobia of this dull room, this suffocating situation, but in the stifling heat of a bedroom ablaze. I'm no longer Evie, I'm her, I'm Bea, my body consumed by flames, smoke filling my lungs so that I can't scream, can't breathe. I feel the chair give way beneath me; hear a crack, then a cry. And then there is a sickening swirl of colour. Lurid oranges and reds devour a peacock blue dress, a pair of silver shoes, the pale fawn of a paperback, until everything is black.

As small children, our greatest fear was waking up with the house on fire. It ranked above being eaten by a giant or torn apart by wolves; a pain terrible and complete. And she would have felt it all.

SEPTEMBER 1987

SHE STANDS *at the crossing on the high road, her impatience swelling like the fast-moving tide of the crowds around her. Cars slow as the lights change and the pedestrians scurry across the sticky tarmac like beetles. But Bea doesn't bustle. Bea walks slowly, savouring each footfall, each revved engine and burst of exhaust fumes, taking in the thick, hot human soup that surrounds her as she reaches New Cross Station.*

This sound, this smell, this feeling is what she has been waiting for. All those long days in stuffy, panelled classrooms reading Coleridge and cutting culottes from an out-of-date pattern; all those long nights in narrow beds in cold dormitories, or running back across dew-damp lawns from some townie's Ford Escort, her face still stinging from his semblance of stubble, the taste of Silk Cut already stale on her lips. They'd all been building up to this moment – to London, to drama school. A week in and she has not tired of it yet. She still sees beauty in the oil patterns in rain-filled gutters and promise in every open doorway.

She'd spent so many hours wishing herself elsewhere. Even at Eden – especially at Eden. At that earthly paradise that Evie so adored she had wasted hours, days willing herself here. "I need to find myself," she'd once said. But even that was a lie, a regurgitation of something she'd heard on a screen at the Lux. She didn't need to find herself; God, you could find anything, anyone in Eden; it was so small, so contained. What she wanted was to be lost, to lose herself in crowds, in life itself. There was a big world out there, one without curfews and cousins, and she wanted to walk in it. To live in it, love in it.

She'd tired of schoolboys with their skintight jeans and studied hairdos. Oh, she'd let them believe she was theirs, for a week, for a night, sucking up their promises and their pathetic adoration, like a thirsty man will drink dirty water. "Do you love me?" she would ask. "Am I beautiful?" And when they said "yes" – for they always did – it would be like a rush of blood to the head and she would feel satisfied for a few dizzying seconds. But it didn't last. She would wake wanting again, needing more praise, more promises. She'd sought out boys that were hard to get, knowing that their affection would mean more once won. Then, that last summer, she'd realized what was right under her nose: Tom; Evie's Tom. And Bea had seduced him with a string bikini, beer, and pouts and pleadings.

She'd been sorry afterwards and had left a letter for Evie to say it was a mistake. But Evie would forgive her; she always did. Anyway, it was over now. She'd left them behind like the detritus of summer – lollipop wrappers and empty bottles and the deserted ice-cream stand. And here, in this breathless, beating city she will find him. The person who will end all that pathetic need, all that fooling around and flirting. She will meet an astonishing boy who will be all things at once: Superman and Lex Luthor – the dashing hero and the complicated, angry poet. And he will make her complete.

She's missed the train into town and must wait for the next one. So she walks to the end of the platform, stands at its tip looking west into the very heart of the city. The metallic tracks gleam amber in the afternoon sun, snaking away from her with all the promise of the yellow brick road and Dick Whittington's streets paved with gold. Like a butterfly unfurling its wings after a chrysalis winter, she spreads her arms and tips her head back, so that the heat and light can fall full on her face.

She's aware then of a sound behind her; no, not a sound, a presence. She opens her eyes, turns her head to see who's there, who is watching her. Of course they're watching. Someone always is.

Then she smiles, for there is not one but two boys – men, even – staring at her. They're not together but she recognizes both of them. She has seen them before around the theatre or in the student bar maybe. One of them leans against a pillar. His arms are tan and lithe, his hair curling round his ears. The other stands a few metres behind him: a paler, ghost-like version of the same. Thin, ethereal almost. Maybe it's one of them, she thinks. Maybe he is the one. And she smiles again: a knowing, goading thing. Then turns back to her reverie, to the yellow road of train tracks.

I am Dorothy, she thinks. I am Dorothy and this is my Oz.

JULY 1988

BEA USED to say that if grief was pie, I'd had a bellyful. A slice for no daddy, or one that wasn't worth keeping. A slice for the mother who died when I was only three from a cancer that grew quickly, so that in two months she'd gone from dancing barefoot on the lawn to being buried in the earth in the village churchyard, leaving me at her childhood home with a handful of costume jewellery and even fewer memories. Another for the beloved grandparents – my guardians – who followed her into the salt-heavy soil when I was ten, orphaning me into the care of an uncle and aunt whose lives were bound to London. So that I was sent scuttling after Bea to boarding school in Berkshire, and Eden became no more than a holiday home. A fourth slice for the affair that cleaved my almost-family in two and meant that Eden would have to be sold soon to pay for the divorce. Four fat pieces of pie that should have filled me to the brim. And they would have done, but for Bea. Because whenever I was sad, whenever I remembered what I'd lost, Bea would take me by the hand and pull me into her bedroom, or down to the creek, whispering secrets and giggling with possibility.

Until she didn't; and now she never would again. Her death was the final flourish – the rotten cherry on top.

The funeral is in the village down river from Eden. I know from lines of overheard conversations between the wobble-armed women cutting crusts off sandwiches in the pantry, from the misplaced confidences of Aunt Julia's sister – Call-Me-Cassie – that my aunt had wanted the funeral near their old house in London, so Bea could lie in the grounds of a grand, show-off church, under a neatly clipped lawn, next to the double-barrelled offspring of Lords or at least hedge-fund managers. But Uncle John has made his one last stand before the decree absolute, and said that Bea's home was always here no matter what Julia might imagine. And so she is coming to Calenick: to the same unpretentious, practical chapel where we buried my mother and grandparents; the same overgrown grave-yard that Bea and I sat in on long, hot Saturdays, sucking Popsicles as we leant on headstones, making up stories about the dead. She will be placed near the same lychgate she kissed Jimmy Fenton under, promising him the world and for ever, and giving him only a feel of her bra strap and a wink on Christmas Eve from the back pew. She came to the graveyard then against Aunt Julia's wishes, just as she's doing now. And she will lie among the undistinguished Trelawneys, Penryns, Cardews instead of the Cadogans or Heath-Watsons of Highgate.

The church is full, its narrow, carved-oak pews packed with Bea's university friends in theatrical hats and wild make-up. The locals are here too, duller in their drab suits and meagre lives, but still clamouring to pay their respects to the girl from the big house. That or pick up gossip. Mrs Polmear from the post office, the Rapsey twins – Joyce and Edna – still living together at the age of fifty-seven, Eddie Maynard from the garage who gave her toffees and bon-bons from the pockets of his overall. Dotted among them are the boys who'd been with her, or wanted to: Jimmy, Eddie's son Luke who worked the petrol pump in stained jeans and an oil-smeared smile, Billy Westcott from the Lugger.

I have a sudden memory of Bea as a child – seven or eight maybe, so I could have been no more than six. We're sat outside the post office, waiting for Grandpa to collect his pension and the racing results from Mrs Polmear, when Bea is struck by the conviction that the shining fragments of mica in the hot pavement are diamonds. She is going to mine them and then make necklaces for us both. She picks away at them, working methodically, determination in her frown and bitten lip, until she releases them from their tar setting and realizes they are no more than dull shards of glass. As disappointing as this motley crew of almost-rans.

But two boys from the list are missing. Two real jewels.

Penn her boyfriend cannot come. His own father is ill – dying, Call-Me-Cassie says. How can he travel when another life hangs in the balance; an important life – an MP? "He doesn't love her," I railed back at her. "He cares more about an old man who's nearly dead anyway." But even as I spit the words out I know it's a lie. Penn loved her. He called Aunt Julia to tell her so, to say how special she was, how lucky he was to have known her, even if only for less than a year.

Of course he loved her. Everyone did. Even Tom.

Why isn't he here? I scour the seats for his familiar slouch, for the hair that falls over his eyes so that he has developed a tic, a constant push to secure it behind his ear for a second before it falls again. But I can't spot him. I don't want to see him anyway, I tell myself. I don't care. I don't need him.

But then I feel it. A change in the light as someone steps from the sun-soaked churchyard into the stony grey of the church. Heads turn and I turn with them, and I see him. He is standing in the doorway between his parents, hair covering downcast eyes, uncomfortable in an ill-fitting suit and someone else's tie. But then he looks up, meets my gaze. And that is when it hits me. The reality of it. Bea is dead.

All my hopes of a mistaken identity – of her appearing at the font demanding to know what on earth we thought we were up to in our gothic lace and black hats without inviting her – dissolve like sugar in the harsh acid of vinegar when I see Tom, when I see that hollow expression, that loss etched on every inch of his face. That is when I swallow the cherry. And feel it drop down and nestle snugly onto the top of four slices of pie, and at the same moment, I feel the world has swallowed me whole.

If the funeral was purgatory, then the wake is hell. Guests swarm over the lawn like ants, clad in the black armour of their mourning clothes, picking at cold meats and cucumber sandwiches and drinking lukewarm wine. I stand on the outskirts, my back against the cedar tree, clutching a glass of flat, tepid Coke like a talisman to ward off well-wishers. Eddie Maynard is heading across the lawn towards me. The three beers inside him and heat of the midday sun are slowing his course and swerving it. I watch him knock into one of the Rapsey twins and, as he over-apologizes, I duck behind the tree, down the path and through the pantry door to peace.

But someone has got there before me.

"Tom?"

"Evie?"

The shock passing over his face becomes something else. Something so potent that I have to put my hand to the countertop to keep myself grounded. I have seen that look before. Last summer, when I ran through the trees to find him and Bea at the creek. The look is guilt.

"What are you doing?" I ask.

"Nothing," he replies, quickly.

"Are you looking for something?" My eyes flick across the room, wondering what it could be that he wants so much. Something of Bea's, maybe, a memento.

But he shakes his head. "Not looking..." He pauses, breathes deeply, as if he has forgotten to until now. "Hiding."

I nod slowly, in reluctant recognition. "Me too."

He smiles at me, a conspiratorial thing, an "I know you, I know what you're feeling". And I feel it then – that ache, that need for him to see me as more than I was; just a friend, almost a sister.

"I can't believe—" he begins.

"Don't," I interrupt.

"Evie, we need to talk. I have to tell you—"

"No. No you don't." I don't want to hear him say her name. I don't want to think about them; don't want to feel that pain in my chest at the way they clung to each other.

"I— I have to go," I stammer. And before he can stop me, I bolt, down the passageway and on through the house. But as my feet clatter up the stairs I realize that running isn't enough, for the second I stop the grief will catch up with me. I need something stronger. More chemical.

The tablets are in the back of Aunt Julia's bedroom drawer. Bea and I found them when we were hunting for adult secrets – for condoms and cigarettes. And they've stayed in the same place ever since, only the date on the prescription changing year to year. I push down the child-proof cap that isn't, turn it and then scatter a handful into my sticky palm, a handful that is too small to miss, but large, still. I count them. Seven. Not enough to die, but enough to lose a week. And with that I swallow a single bitter pill.

AUGUST 1987

SEAMUS LIES *on the now-faded, outdated Superman of his duvet cover, eyes closed, one arm flung back like the flying hero, the opening chords of "Last Night I Dreamt..." filling the four walls of the attic. His mam had bought him this bed-set and he'd refused to part with it all these years, even now at the age of eighteen.*

The day of his mam's funeral, Seamus was nine. The only boy of five live births, he sat on the pew at the front of Our Lady of Lourdes, wedged in between two of his big sisters, the nylon of his borrowed blazer chafing his newly shaved neck. He reached up to scratch and his elbow knocked into Brigid's left breast.

"Ow."

He felt the lightning-quick dig of an eleven-year-old elbow in retort. Sharp and deliberate, it jabbed into his ribs, pushing him into Theresa who was flanking him on the other side.

"Bloody hell, Seamus. Quit mithering," she snapped, her hand flying to her hair to check the Silvikrin was doing its job, that the painstakingly styled flicks were still in place. "Or e'll 'ave you," she added pointlessly.

Seamus looked frantically down the row, but his father was five seats away. An unbreachable gap of uniform-clad sisters and his Aunty Maureen, weeping noiselessly into an ironed handkerchief, lay between them.

His dad had patted his shoulder that morning. Not the usual "Jesus, will ya get out of the way" swipe. But a lighter, "it'll be fine, just don't bloody cry" touch. That was the closest he'd ever been to his father – as a sickly infant, in and out of St Augustine's so often the cleaners knew him by sight, by the sound of his mewling cry; as a mud-dirtied scabbed-kneed littl'un; throughout his mam's trouble – and it was the closest he'd ever get. That gap of four women had widened by the passing of years. Grammar school, music – Echo and the Bunnymen, The Cure, The Smiths, make-up – an eyeliner and nail polish hocked from Brigid's dressing table, and, finally, the arrival of Deirdre Eckersley from Gidlow Street and another sister to add her whine to the clamouring throng, had all increased the gulf.

Deirdre is nothing like his mam. No singing along to Bonnie Tyler on Radio 2 while she washes up seven sets of breakfast bowls. No Fairy-soft hand riffling his hair at the tea table, laughing away his indignation at stew, promising him jam on his rice pudding if he eats it all up. No lips brushing his ear at bedtime, whispering in a faint Cork lilt that he mustn't worry what his da says, that he is her special boy, that he will go so far in life, fly so high, that he will have to wear a suit to protect him from the sun, will need binoculars to look back down at her from his giddy heights.

No, Deirdre is nothing like that. She is hard corners and sharp words. No soft hands from the dishwater. That is his job now. No soft talk, just an "eat it or you know what you'll get" at tea, and a knock on the wall and "turn out that bloody light" at bedtime. He is not her special boy. He will not go far. He will end up in bloody borstal if he carries on the way he is. Holy Mary, Mother of God, what does he think he is playing at?

But he knows exactly what he's playing at.

He's alone in this humdrum town, he understands that now. In the cream-gloss, chalk-dust corridors of the grammar, on the steamed-up top deck of the 72 bus with its back-seat snogging and illicit trade in sweets and cigarettes and dirty magazines, in this jerry-built house of bar heaters and bare floorboards.

But down south, just three hundred miles and three weeks away, is another life. One with conversations that don't feature United or Athletic or racing. One with shelves filled with Keats and Yeats instead of Reader's Digest. One with *supper, not cheap-as-chippy tea; wine, not bitter; and Pears soap instead of the acrid, yellowing bars of coal tar that Deirdre makes him wash with, wash his mouth out with. This life will be his for the taking. Drama school in London. Where he will take the lead, be centre stage, be the boy his ma knew he could be. Where he'll no longer be Seamus, but James. A man of class, of means, of mystery. Like James Bond, like James Dean.*

The song is over, its three-minute perfection fading to static. Seamus holds himself in its comforting hum until the talking and walking and eating and evacuating that continues around him in a ceaseless, mindless cycle in this house of cards penetrates the paper-thin walls of his room. He hears Brigid singing tunelessly along to a song in her head, by some vacuous pop star that she has fallen hopelessly, irrevocably in love with, until next week. Hears the rhythmic thud, thud of his half sister Siobhan jumping rope in her room. Hears the bang, bang, bang of Deirdre banging her broom handle on the ceiling in retort. Hears the shuddering stop of his da's Transit van outside. This van, with its slipping clutch, choking exhaust, and back full of valves and ballcocks and plastic piping, is promised to him one day; a day his da can proudly add "& son" to the decal "Gillespie" on the back and sides.

A day that they both secretly, silently, know will never come.

The van door clunks shut, and a few seconds later the front door slams in echo. And then the sounds of the house

alter to accommodate this incomer. The skipping and sing-
ing come to a faltering halt to be replaced by the rattle of the
chip pan and the clatter of frozen fishfingers onto the grill
tray. Then the TV is flicked on, the petty arguments start and
Seamus drops the needle back on the record and lets Mor-
rissey and Marr drown out the disappointment of this flock-
papered, broken-biscuit, so-called life.

JULY 1988

THE PILLS ran out three days ago. The last satisfying, slow descent into a place devoid of sharp feelings, where hard edges are blurry, soft as cotton wool, where I am comfortably numb. Now, as I lie awake on my bed in the room Bea and I shared, I see everything. I hear everything.

Eden is almost empty. Like a rat from a sinking ship Uncle John fled to the city after the funeral. Someone called Harry had phoned with an emergency, and they couldn't do without him. And now there is only Aunt Julia, Call-Me-Cassie, and me.

And Bea.

I hear her. I see her everywhere. The thud of a hardback book slipping from her hand onto the faded cabbage-rose carpet. Her soft breathing when I would wake early on summer mornings, roused by the crack of sunlight across my pillow, while she, shaded, slept on past breakfast. Her leg dangling from beneath a tangled sheet, fishing for cooler air, the toenails a chipped scarlet stolen from Aunt Julia's dresser, matching my own. Always matching. Matching pirouetting ballerina pillowcases, matching custard-yellow candlewick covers, matching mule slippers we begged for from Dingles in Plymouth, that flick-flacked so satisfyingly on the flagstone floors.

"Paper dolls" they used to call us: cut from the same tall, pale sheet. Our legs measured exactly twenty-nine inches, as if mine had defied their two-year disadvantage and determinedly grown to equal hers. Our noses were freckled in the same spattering pattern, though she had thirty-seven, and I forty-three. Our hair bobbed to our chins in an identical shade of brown. Somehow the few genes we shared through my mother and her father had conspired to make up for our lack of siblings and blue-printed instead into cousins.

My grandfather said I was a loner as a child. But I wasn't, not really. I was just in a sort of limbo, a without-Bea time, when I got on with the long business of waiting for Aunt Julia to bring her back here for the holidays so that the world could start turning again. Even at school I preferred to play my own private hopscotch rather than join in the noisy games of tag or stuck-in-the-mud or kick-the-can. For why would I want to chase and be chased by girls who weren't as brilliant, or bright, or beautiful as Bea? No, I would wait until Bea returned and then I would teach her all I had learned – to catch pollack from the harbour wall, to body surf the waves that crashed onto the gritty sand of the cove. And she in turn would teach me to plait my hair, paint kohl on my eyelids, to French kiss my pillow in practice for the real thing.

Until one day she didn't.

I feel a surge of nausea as the truth I have dampened down is now borne by butterflies, bright, glistening into the air: I didn't lose Bea in the fire. Nor even last summer when she kissed Tom, and then left for college in London. The truth is she had already slipped away from me.

It started when she was fifteen years old and I just fourteen. She'd been to stay with a school friend – Kate Flint, "Flinty", who had a perm and a parrot called Longjohn, and whom I loathed and admired in equal measure. When Bea returned, eight days, ten hours and seventeen minutes later, she was laden with three things: a copy of *Lace*, ten plastic bangles that clattered annoyingly up and down her arms whenever she moved, and the faded purple of a bruise just above her right shoulder.

At first I felt delight, that she and Flinty had fought like children, that their tight-knit affair was unravelling. "Oh, Evie, it's not a bruise," she laughed. "It's a hickey."

She told me about him. His name was Miles, the best friend of the brother of Flinty's friend Ruby Woo. He was a whole year older, and a whole twenty pages of the *Teen Guide to Relationships* more experienced. She whispered the words across the four-foot-wide strip of carpet and discarded socks and battered books that separated our beds. Yet that night it felt as wide as the Atlantic. Because, while I lapped up the story like sweet sugar slush, it left a bitter aftertaste on my tongue, for I knew she'd said it all before. That Flinty had heard it first in fuller, more lurid detail, had giggled with her over the practised way he undid her bra, gasped that he'd asked her to touch his "thing", clapped her hands together at their ill-thought-out promise to duck school and meet under the clock at Waterloo on the first Friday in October.

And so it began. The paper-thin sliver of air between us became a gaping chasm that widened on a weekly basis: The time she had her ear pierced twice in the back-street salon in Plymouth while I lay shivering in bed with unseasonal flu. The time she "forgot" we'd said we'd paint the boathouse door cherry red, like Madonna's lips, and I came down to the creek to see a half-finished mess of pea green and Bea inside with a boatbuilder's boy called Cal. The time she didn't come for the holidays at all. Went to Switzerland to spend two weeks in a chalet with Greta Johansson and her two brothers, and a ski instructor called Nils.

And the things we shared – our skinny, boy-thin bodies, our wide lips, our pale-as-milk skin – disappeared, disguised under so many layers of ra-ra skirts and

Maybelline mascara and a lipstick named Twilight Teaser. Until her things – her new make-up, her new clothes, her new self – became too much for our childish room with its twin wooden beds and yellow spreads and circus-themed wallpaper. And so Aunt Julia moved her to the attic, to an ivory tower and canopied double bed, where she could whisper under the covers with the endless stream of schoolfriends – the Hatties and Letties and Charlie-not-Charlottes who were driven down for the sea air, and the swimming, and the novelty of village boys. While I was left behind with her childish toys; her rejects.

I stare at Bea's old bed and the menagerie of stuffed animals that still colonizes it – three grey rabbits with pale silk ears, a worn plush monkey, a real-fur koala with a hard plastic nose and scratchy toes. They stare glassily back at me like a malevolent zoo. I shiver, with cold, or something else, sadness maybe. I can't stay here, here with the circus on the walls and the zoo on the bed and the No Bea. I slip out of bed and pad along the landing, my bare feet instinctively avoiding the boards that creak or crack under pressure; a path mapped fastidiously by Bea and me years ago to avoid capture by pirates or monsters, or worse, Aunt Julia.

At the end of the landing, I turn, and start the steep, narrow climb to the attic. The door is shut, has been shut since Bea's last visit home from college last year. I feel the ridges of the beehived handle rough in my palm, then turn it slowly, and push.

There is no phantom, no brush of gossamer shroud against me, only a gasp of stale air, as if the room has been holding its breath. But as it exhales I feel my own lungs stopper up. There's no need to turn on the light; the moon shows me all I need to see: The mirror, obscured now by only a thin curtain of beads and ribbons, those that were not taken to London. Knickers still spilling out of the drawer, a froth of lace and coloured silk. Make-up spilling across the dresser top, nail polish dripping onto the floor, great gobs of blood red on the pale carpet. The unmistakeable cloying note of her bottle of White Musk. And a book – a battered board-covered edition of *Peter Pan*.

We never stopped loving that story. We played for hours at being Peter and Wendy, Hook and the tick-tocking crocodile, the insolent Tinkerbell. Yet we both knew that really we were the Lost Boys, raised by Eden, and by an array of Wendys – the housekeepers my grandfather employed; my infant school teacher Mrs Penrice; Hannah – Tom's mother, and my own mother's friend.

I put my hand on the dresser to steady myself and feel it knock something to the floor. When I stoop to retrieve it I see it is an unopened letter addressed to Bea. I don't recognize the writing, our address mapped out in a deep, blue-black ink, the loops extravagant yet exact. I check the postmark: Hampshire. Hampshire, I think, Hampshire. I know someone who lives there. I dig into my head, poke fingers into dark recesses. And that's when I see it: the date. This isn't an old letter. This letter was sent the day that Bea died.

I sit on the edge of her princess-and-the-pea bed, the envelope crackling in my hand. I wrestle with myself for pointless seconds before the need to read the letter beats any reason not to and I slide a finger under the flap and open it in one clean, swift rip.

Cobham House
Wick Lane
Tetlow
Hampshire

6th July 1988

Bea

I'm so sorry. I'm a fool. I've always known that. Only you – beautiful trusting you – didn't see it, or maybe you just refused to, chose to overlook it. But I know you can't overlook this, and I don't want you to. I deserve to be punished. But I want – hope – that I can persuade you I deserve forgiveness too. What happened – that was the old Penn. The one I was before I met you and you changed my world, and changed me. I got scared I was losing you, that's all.

But Bea, I can't lose you. You haven't just changed my world, you ARE my world. And I want to be yours

37

again. I want to be everything to you and do every-
thing with you. I'm glad you've gone home, in an odd
way. Because now I'll get to go there too. I want to
see Eden while I still can. I want to meet Evie. Is she
like you? I hope so. There should be more people like
you – a thousand Beas. But you will always be the
original. The most-Bea of all.

I'm writing nonsense now, aren't I? Oh, Bea, I
have to talk to you. I called but no one's answering
the phone. Call me when you get this and I'll explain
and I'll beg and I'll apologize and you can make me
suffer all you want as long as you agree to see me. And
then I'll come. As soon as I can, I promise, I'll come.

I love you
Penn xxx

I read it only once. Once is enough to know how much he
loved her, and she loved him. And I feel a strange satisfaction, a relief even, that she told him about me.

But it's not that which makes my heart suspend its
frantic rhythm for a single beat. It's that Bea was coming
home, to Eden.

I feel the grief mixed with the guilt come over me slowly. If I'd written back to her, if I'd told her I forgive her,
would she have come sooner? Would she still be alive? Or
would she see through the lie it was?

A tremor at first, distant and deep, then with only this
faintest of warnings it washes through me, over me like a

tidal wave. I am helpless before it and begin to sob, great heaving racks that judder through my body. I cry until the salt stings my cheeks, until snot tangles in my hair, until I cannot breathe, cannot see, cannot weep any more. And then, in her bed, I fall into a black, dreamless sleep.

AUGUST 1987

PENN HANGS *over the side of his too-small bed in this too-big house in Hampshire. Lets the blood fill his head until he can hear it singing in his ears, until it drowns out the noise and the nausea. He opens his eyes and sees a used condom, a flaccid thing like a shed snakeskin. Was there a girl here? Is there a girl here? He reaches with one leg, sweeps it delicately across the sheets. Nothing.*

But there was. Yes, he can see her now. Or parts of her: slivers of her skin, dark against his own; the blue-black gloss of her hair, like the wing of a starling; the scar on her thigh, a red, angry worm. Though he can't recall her name or her face with any precision.

He hauls himself up then, reaches for the Zippo and the

remains of a spliff sat fatly among the ashes on the bedside table.

He's still smoking when the door opens and his father appears, stone-faced and sweating in his immaculate suit and old school tie.

"I suppose they all do it, smoke this – this stuff, do they?" he says finally. "These new friends of yours. These theatre people." He spits the word out as if it is poison.

Penn sighs, stubs it out, shrugs. "No."

The room fills with a silence heavier than smoke. It will suffocate them both if someone does not speak soon.

It is his father who gives in first, as it always is. "You're wasting your time," he says, for the fourth time that summer. "I offered you that job at the Commons. Low wages I know, for now. But think where it would lead."

Penn stares at the ceiling, half listens as his father lists the golden opportunities he is throwing away, snubbing, as if they were no more than a paper round or a Saturday job at the butcher's: the glittering people he will meet, the glittering career he could have, the chance of a seat of his own someday. He gets louder, more desperate with each offering, until he dissolves into a fit of rattling coughing.

"You should get that checked out," Penn says, as his father retrieves his ironed handkerchief from his inside pocket and wipes his brow, his mouth.

"Don't tell me what to do," the man retorts, his florid face deepening to a still darker red.

"Then don't tell me," Penn replies.

Penn is still gazing at the fringing on the lampshade an hour later. He doesn't know why he is still here, or why he came back here from college in the first place. Duty, maybe? Or habit. Or the lure of a summer in the country with a swimming pool and local girls drawn to its blue like butterflies. Like flies.

Not that he's been near the thing. Doesn't even like to swim. Instead he's been stuck indoors, stifling in the heat and under the weight of expectation as his father tries to construct an alternative future for him within his own strict parameters: doctor, lawyer, MP. And Penn, in defiance, has stepped backwards, retreated into women, into wine, into whatever will take him out of this straitjacketed world.

He will change though. Because he's not what his father says. He's not a wastrel. He has talent; has been told this time and time again. People want to be him – have told him so in vodka-soaked plaudits at parties. He would roll his eyes, take an overblown bow, and ride on this brief burst of public glory. But then later, alone in his room, on his bed, the drink worn off and the applause long faded, he would wish he were anyone but himself. Wish he'd been born a different boy, to a different father, and a different world. No one understands that. Not the others on his course, nor any of the women he has whispered his hopes to.

But someone will. And when he finds her, he will keep her.

JULY 1988

I AWAKE to disappointment. To the reality, the stark-ness that daylight reveals in its unrelenting rise and fall. To the realization that my crying wasn't cathartic, that giving into grief – one self-indulgent session of pity and pathos – didn't exorcize the ghost. As I sit up in her bed, in her room, in her world, I'm still shocked and confused, and I feel her more than ever.

I read the letter again – Penn's letter. A night hasn't diminished its content, lessened its meaning. She was coming home. She was coming home – even though she swore she'd never bother again, said her life was in London now and would always be.

So why didn't she come?

I want a cigarette.

We've smoked since she was fourteen and I twelve, learning from the village boys on the harbour walls and behind the pub, practising in the boathouse with Silk Cut borrowed from Aunt Julia. "She'll think she smoked them herself," said Bea confidently. "You have to smoke to be an actress anyway. It's a career advancement." And then she would blow smoke rings, looking for all the world like a schoolgirl Dietrich.

The first time I tried it, it tasted of stale biscuits and left me coughing and green-faced. It wasn't until we were back at school that I realized the importance of cigarettes and saw the meetings on the back field to which entry was gained only by ownership of a lighter or the ability to French inhale. And so I learnt, forcing myself to manage half a Marlboro Light at a time without throwing up. Not to fit in, but so as not to lose out, to lose Bea. That way I could at least skirt at the edges of her circle. I never smoked any on my own.

And now, this morning, I crave it; the rush of nicotine, the defiance of knowing self-destruction. But I have none, and Julia, of course, has given up.

But Bea always had cigarettes – in her bag, in her pockets, in various drawers and boxes, stashed amongst the lipsticks, letters and condoms; the detritus of a life lived loved. I push my hand to the back of the drawer and strike gold – a packet of Player's, quarter-full, and a Bic lighter, a millilitre of fluid still visible in its pale blue transparency.

Bea was last here at Christmas. She managed three days from Christmas Eve to Boxing Day before begging Uncle John for a lift to the station, vowing never to come back. Seven months ago since she opened these.

Seven months since she spoke to me. Barely spoke. Or rather that was me. "How's Tom?" she asked. I paused, snorted incredulously, then spat out a calculated, spiteful "Like you care." I regretted the words even as their shape was still on my lips. I regret them infinitely, incalculably, now. Such a pointless row, a waste of words, of time we could have been together, truly together. And over what? A boy she'd never loved, and who had never loved me?

I tap a cigarette out of the packet, then climb up onto the window seat beneath the dormer, open the casement wide and light it up. The harsh smoke catches my throat but I stifle the urge to cough for fear of waking Julia, then, as it eases, I breathe out slowly, and look out over Eden.

This has been my kingdom for as long as I can remember. The lawns, studded by dark, gleaming rhododendrons and edged by the darker-still woods, the corrugated iron of the boathouse roof and the glimpse of water beyond, tantalizing in its sun-silvered brightness. Yet she didn't notice this. When she looked down from this vaunted perch, I believe she saw only the sea beyond, a world so vast and infinite that she couldn't wait to be out in it, to find every corner, taste every new sensation, wring every last drop of life from it. While me – all I wanted was here.

They begged her not to leave, or not go to London

anyway, fought her decision to do drama, said she should pick something sensible – law or medicine or maths – and at Oxford, surely, or Durham at least. Said it would be for her own good. But it wouldn't have been. She'd have withered, died in those stuffy, dust-filled places, studying numbers or anatomy or anything that demanded such precision, such measured silence.

Yet, even knowing this, I fought too. And my reasons were just as selfish. I knew it was the end of it all, of the parting that had begun at school and quickened the summer of the lovebite. She knew it too.

"But it will be an awfully big adventure, Evie," she had said, quoting Pan triumphantly and smiling with the promise of it all. "Remember?"

I shook my head. "No," I replied, grimly. "You've got it wrong. The awfully big adventure? That's 'death'."

She shrugged. "Well, either way, it's better than here."

I start at the sudden quick turn of the door handle. I'm not practised like Bea was – adept at disguising the smell and hiding the fag ends in a matter of well-timed seconds – so that when Aunt Julia enters it is into the unmistakeable fug of smoke and the sight of me hurling a hastily stubbed-out cigarette butt onto the gravel below. Her face is drawn, grey; valium and Clarins failing to cover her age and grief and this new disappointment.

"For God's sake." She stalks over and opens a second window, throwing it wide so that it clanks dangerously against the granite, threatening to shatter. "It'll kill you."

"I wish it would," I retort. And then we both realize what I've said. The fire that killed Bea could have been started by a cigarette – Bea's cigarette. The words sour on my tongue.

"I don't want the house smelling of smoke," Aunt Julia says stiffly.

"You're still selling?" I demand. "After this? After everything?"

Aunt Julia looks down, at some scuff on the skirting board, real or imagined, then busies herself picking up a sock, a pair of tights. "Of course," she continues. "We can't stay. You know that. We can't afford it."

I know that, but I don't like it.

"But you can't," I plead. "It's ours – mine, I mean." Which it is; left to Bea and me by our grandfather who knew his own son and daughter-in-law never loved it like he did, like I did.

"You'll get your share," she says. Her voice is tight now, nearly snapping, her knuckles white as she grips the sock. "Bea's reverts to John and me."

I pause, then load a final rounded stone into my slingshot, take aim and fire: "She wouldn't have wanted this."

But though it ruffles the air as it flies, the shot falls short and rolls slowly, harmlessly under a cupboard. Because we both know that's not true. She had outgrown Eden years ago. It was only me who clung on.

SEPTEMBER 1987

THE GIRL *is standing with her back to Penn, arms wide, facing the west of the city, letting the late afternoon light fall on her face. A halo of gold flickers around her hair and fingertips, and in her pale, net-skirted dress she could be an earthly angel.*

She turns her head swiftly, suddenly, as if she can feel his gaze hot on her like the sun. And he can see her face now; her wide, dark eyes; her pale skin; her cheeks and lips stained pink with the flush of knowing she is watched.

This isn't the first time Penn has seen her. He's counted up the moments like a small child with birthday coins. Once in the foyer of the theatre on her audition day five months ago, when she wore Doc Martens and a band in her hair, like

a strange, overgrown Alice in Wonderland. Once outside the
accommodation office last week, a suitcase in one hand and
her new key in the other, smiling like she was about to enter
a rococo palace, not a concrete new-build off Lewisham Way.
Once in the bar, barefoot, a country girl airdropped in the big
city; yet not lost, she never looks lost. And now here, today.

The East London line train pulls in and the girl climbs
aboard, and even though Penn is waiting for another train,
to take him to Charing Cross and his father, even though this
will take him miles and minutes, maybe hours out of his way,
he follows her.

"You're Bea," he says, flopping down in the seat next to
her, his face spreading into a wide Cheshire-cat smile.

She looks up from her book lazily. "And how would you
know that?"

"I asked around."

"Following me, were you?"

She pretends to read, but he can see that her eyes don't
move over the lines and her cheeks are creased with a smile,
and he knows she is rapt by him, not Gatsby.

"What if I were?" he tests.

She drops the book, puts one hand on her chest in mock
fear. "Then I'd scream rape and my bodyguards would appear
as if by magic. And then, well, I can't go into details but you
wouldn't like it."

"Have a drink with me," he says.

"Now?"

"Why not."

"I'm meeting someone. A girl," she adds. "We're going to a play, at the Half Moon. A Dario Fo thing, it's called—"

"Elizabeth," he finishes for her.

"You've seen it?"

"Last week. Compulsory thing. I'm doing political comedy for my final year."

"You're a drama student?"

"Goldsmiths," he says. "But then you knew that."

She laughs, caught out. "I did," she nods. "But don't read too much into it. Everyone knows you."

"So you know I'm not dangerous. Ditch the play; come with me."

The train slows, pulls to a stop. "Maybe another time," she smiles.

And with that promise on her lips and a book in her hand, she flits, bird-like, before he can think of anything else to say.

JULY 1988

AND SO they come to Eden. Men in dirt- and time-stained overalls pack up half our world in cardboard boxes so that the decorators can come and paint away the last traces of our lives. The portraits on the stairs of long-dead relatives bearing pieces of me and Bea – our lips, our eyes, our noses – are the first to go. Oil likenesses of long-dead men and women in awkward clothes and forced poses are bubble-wrapped ready for auction, their stories reduced to a few lines in a catalogue. Then curtains are taken down, dust sheets draped over chaise longues and wing-backed chairs and the drop-leaf table in the drawing room that served as our fortress.

But I can't be packed in a box to be sold off or

squirrelled into storage. Instead I shut myself in my room, hoping that if I'm quiet enough they will leave me behind. I'm fooling myself, I know. But I'm determined, will hold out until the bitter, inevitable end. I eat toast, cereal, soup left at the door by Aunt Julia; pee in the sink, using the bathroom only late at night when I can steal unnoticed the few steps along the corridor.

Call-Me-Cassie leaves but I mumble a goodbye from behind the bolted door.

Hannah – Tom's mum – calls, bringing cookies and concern, but I send her away, throw the biscuits in the bin. I'd choke on love if I tried to eat one.

But a day later Tom comes, and Julia knocks on my door.

"I don't want to see him," I protest. "I don't want to see anyone."

"He's not anyone," retorts Aunt Julia. "He's your friend."

He is. Was. He was the one who taught me to fish, to dive, to row. He was my without-Bea-time friend. Until one day I fell swiftly, hopelessly in love, and he became so much more. And then, just as quickly, so much less.

I don't know how it changed, or why, only that it did. That somehow, as we lay on the deck of the pontoon, side by side, our noses peeling, our voices cracking with laughter as we sang "Hey Frankie" to the butcher's boy Frank Delaney fishing in the shallows, he became my world. So that every stretch of bare arm and leg became something forbidden, every smile left me breathless with want. Until I no longer felt safe, solid, grounded, in his presence but instead sensed a strange, teetering vertigo, as if I might fall at any minute from a great height. If only he would catch me.

And I imagined this. Oh, I imagined it. That I would stumble, faint, like some fey, corseted ingénue. And he would catch me, his face etched with concern as he willed my eyes to open. And then, when they did, he would gaze into them, lower his face until our lips touched and we would dissolve into unnamable, unimaginable bliss.

I searched for any hint that he felt the same, would dissect our every encounter for a trace of a touch left lingering a second too long, a glance at my breasts, a shy look away. But I unearthed nothing. "He must be gay," I told myself. Or, worse, in love with someone else. But who? For I would know about her, surely? He would have told me, like he told me about the time he kissed Sally Mackinnon behind the bike shed but she tasted of orange Tic Tacs and he's never eaten them since.

Unless, unless...

And then that wretched hot day, I stumbled upon the truth that I'd not dared to admit. That it was Bea he wanted, Bea he must have reserved his glances for, and I – blinded by love or desperation – had failed to see them.

So no, I don't want to see him.

Aunt Julia sends him up anyway. "Talk some sense into her," I imagine her saying. And he tries.

He knocks, says my name. "Evie?" His voice is deeper than I remember, rougher somehow, and I picture his hand, the whorls on his fingertips worn from the ropes on the ferry he tills at weekends, the palms blackened with oil from the outboard engine; his hair, longer now, a curtain drawn over his eyes so that he can peer out but no one can look in.

I hear a sound, the "shhh" of shoe rubber turning on carpet, and think he's given up. But just as I reach to clasp my pathetic victory, I hear something else, a swish of cotton against wood, the rattle of a lock. He hasn't fled. He's sat down, back against the door, and it's one–all.

"I'm worried about you," he says.

Nothing.

"We all are."

Nothing.

"I miss you."

I feel something tighten inside my stomach. A knot of anger. Or hurt. "Miss her, you mean."

"No— Yes. Of course… But you too. Last summer… Bea, I didn't… I mean, it wasn't. She was just… "

I mumble, a formless noise that sounds like disbelief, but even I can hear it is wrapped in something else. Hope, maybe. And then I say it. Say the thing I have wanted to, have wanted to shout at him, scream at him. But it comes out as barely a whisper.

"You kissed her," I say.

"No. I—"

"I saw you," I say, louder now. "I saw you with her."

"Yes, but— I didn't…" He pauses, trying to concoct

some answer, I think – something more palatable. "Evie, she kissed me, OK? Bea kissed me. Not the other way round."

I snort. But then, hoping, I think back to what I saw, the tangle of arms, the confusion of sounds. But it's no good. As hard as I try I can still see them, see the truth of it: his hand reaching to her face, his fingers on her cheek, that sound that he made, not of disgust but of pleasure, I am sure of it.

"But you let her."

He's silent for a moment. Thinking up a lie, maybe.

"At first. But then…" he trails off. "Shit. I should've talked to you about it at Christmas. But you wouldn't see me."

"Oh, it's my fault?" I shoot back. Though I feel the truth hit me as sharp as a stone.

"No, I … that's not what I'm saying."

"It doesn't matter," I add. "It's not like I care."

"Evie…"

"I don't," I lie. "It's done."

Then we fall into awkward, deafening silence.

"I'm sorry," he says eventually.

"What for?"

"I don't know, everything I guess. That. Bea. The house…" He pauses. "I can't believe you're going."

"Me neither," I say to myself. Though I've known for a year now. That though my grandfather bequeathed us the house he left no money to run it. That even without the divorce it would have to be sold, or leased out. Bea shrugged when she was told, but her world was vast, and losing a corner of it was small change. But my world was here and I begged Aunt Julia to change her mind, to run it as a B & B, or an art school. I'd read about one in Tregony, a fading manor that had been brought back to life by week-long courses in watercolour. But Julia couldn't bear the thought of more than a few months at a time in this "godforsaken place". Everything I loved, she hated; the solitude, the isolation, the silence. She couldn't see the attraction of long walks and log fires and beds that needed warming with copper pans or rubber bottles before you could climb into them. "What about Hannah?" I would ask. "She was from London." "Well, yes," my aunt would reply, "but she's different." Poor, she meant. A sculptress, she'd been a friend of my mother's at art college. She came down for a holiday after graduation and fell in love; with the river, with Eden, with a young carpenter called Bill who lived in the Millhouse, and never left. And now there is Tom, and a garden full of bronze hares and minotaurs. And no money. But love.

"Remember when we broke the sofa in the morning room?" he asks.

I smile at the sudden memory. It was years ago – five, maybe more. We were trying to fly; bouncing off the base to see who could get highest, furthest across the carpet and onto a pile of cushions. A game that lasted for hours before ending with the crack of old wood and a shriek from Tom, whose ankle was trapped in old webbing.

"You cried," I say, remembering now.

"Only a bit," he says. "More from pride than pain."

Part of me wants to make him laugh, then tease out other memories – the time we tried to dye ourselves blue in the bath; the time Bea and I cut Tom's hair with pinking shears; the time we drew an army of animals marching along the scullery wall; the time we stole a bowl of chocolate mousse intended for a dinner party and ate it all with our fingers before being sick in turns on the back lawn.

But then everything comes back to that day, the last time we were together, and I know I can't do it because all those other times, those memories, are sullied, dirtied. They were charades, I think, and only that last day was real.

"When do you leave?" he asks.

"Aunt Julia goes in two days," I say, by way of an answer.

And then there is silence again, silence that stretches into minutes, then half an hour.

"I should go," he says.

"Sure," I say.

"See you soon."

I shrug, then realizing he can't see me add, "I doubt it."

Three words, again. Three words I want to erase, to rub out like our pencil marks on the scullery walls, because the anger that bore them isn't at him, not really. It's at the end of it all: of Bea, of us, of Eden. I wanted one last summer here. No, *want* one last summer. I want her to fill my head, my heart, with her wild ideas, her unfailing conviction. I want to play in this paradise, fading though it is. Not just because Eden belongs to me but because I belong to it.

I don't want to go to the new flat in London. I don't want to be in the big wide world that Bea talked about. I want to be here. This is my world.

It comes over me like warm syrup on porridge, a sweet realization: I have to stay. Just for a few weeks. Until I find out how to be without her – to be me without her.

I'm going to stay at Eden. Somehow, I'm going to stay.

OCTOBER 1987

COLLEGE IS *more like school than James had imagined.*
The same tired teachers repeating last year's lessons; the same
ranks wide-eyed, like it's the Sermon on the Mount, all be-
lieving these words hold the key to their transformation into
the Next Big Thing; the same self-appointed monarchy rul-
ing over the also-rans, a caste system based on no more than
who has the loudest voice, or the most famous father, or the
best dope – a crown he knows he can never claim for his own
and so doesn't bother to covet.

She is different, though.

He thought she'd made a mistake when she walked into
the auditorium that first afternoon and stood squinting up at
the raked seats, her hand shielding her eyes against the glare

of the stage lights. He assumed she'd been looking for a friend, or for another lecture hall at the far end of the campus where the literature students gathered, crow-like in their black coats and boots. He thought it couldn't possibly be this easy, that she would be thrown into his path like this. But then a name was called and she answered with "here".

"Bea." He says it in his head. Then out loud, savouring the way it feels in his mouth; its rounded perfection, like an egg.

Bea. Bee. A buzzing bright queen, she soars above them all, refuses to align herself with the lesser insects. James feels it; the authenticity of her. None of Theresa or Brigid's bottled bronze or frosted gloss. No fakery or fraudulence like the girls on the bus, the pretenders and wannabes in their black-market Chanel and straight-off-the-market nylon. None of the desperation of the other girls on the course, who want to be Hepburn or Redgrave or Rossellini. He watches her with that girl Hetty with the Louise Brooks bob, with the two Lucys who wear such similar black uniforms he forgets which is which, with those third years that cluster around Penn. She flits in and out of their circles on gossamer wings, like the angel he saw at the station that day. No, not an angel, a fairy; Puck or Ariel, or Tinkerbell even, dancing around the Lost Boys. And he, he is Peter Pan.

Then one evening in the bar when Hetty is arguing about Page 3 girls at a Women's Soc meeting and Penn and the others are playing pinball with a devotion usually reserved for international sport – she lands next to him.

* * *

He's sat at a table in the corner, a paperback copy of The
Tempest *in one hand, in the other a pint of Flowers he has
nursed for one long hour already, and will make last another
before he makes the walk back down Queens Road and home.
He'd thought he'd drink wine by now, a claret or burgundy.
But beer is cheaper, lasts longer.*

*He's auditioning soon and is lost on Prospero's island
when the tide washes her ashore and she drops into the worn
leatherette next to him and says, "Which part are you going
for?"*

He starts, drops the book, apologizes.

*But she doesn't roll her eyes or drift away. She picks it
up for him, wipes a film of beer off on her dress. One small,
simple act of kindness, of selflessness. But for James it is
everything.*

*"Prospero," he says, taking it back from her. "Though I
won't get it."*

"You don't know that."

"Penn will get it. Everyone thinks so."

*"Then everyone is wrong. Because Penn's not going for
it," she replies with a raised eyebrow. "But don't say I said so."*

*"He's not?" He's not sure whether to be happier with this
pearl of knowledge, or that she chose to reveal it to him alone.*

*"He's got too much on," she smiles. "I heard him tell
Hunter. Stuff at home, too, you know?"*

*He nods. Though he can't imagine what "stuff" Penn
would have. Penn didn't come from a back-to-back in Wigan,*

the son of a plumber. Penn was born with a silver spoon in his mouth, not coal tar soap to wash out the swearing.

"I love the magic plays," she says then. "When I was little I used to pretend I was Miranda and wait for Ferdinand to rescue me."

"And did he?"

"Not yet," she smiles slowly and bites her lip.

And in those two words he knows what she is telling him. That he has a chance, that if he is special enough, brave enough, she could be his.

"Though in truth I think he's a bit of a drip," she continues. "It's Caliban who gets the best lines, don't you think?"

"Yes!" he agrees emphatically. "Yes, I do."

And that is how the conversations begin. Conversations wound through with importance, with meaning. Conversations he tells himself they will remember not just when they wake in the morning, but when they lie in bed when they are old. Conversations about the miners, about Thatcher, about the future of theatre and the history of everything.

They talk through another pint in the NUS bar, then two in the Rosemary Branch on the New Cross Road.

They talk all the way from the pub, past the late night minimart and the shuttered junk shops, up the hill to Lawrence Hall, where she lives.

"So, this is it," she says.

"This is it," he repeats.

And then there is a pause, a moment that dances with possibility; but in the seconds it takes for him to summon the courage, she turns and is gone, the fire door slamming shut on her retreating figure as she winds her way up the communal stairs, leaving him to the sodium glow of the streetlight and the sirens of late-night Lewisham.

JULY 1988

SO I make a plan to stay. A blueprint built on desperation, and held clumsily together with the Sellotape that is the self-belief of youth; a whip-smart answer to every "what if" or "but" Aunt Julia could throw at me, and a final flourish, a triumphant trump card: I wasn't doing this for me, I was doing it for her.

I've worked it all out: when she goes back to the flat in London, returns to her coffee mornings and tea parties and cocktails at seven, I will stay here and supervise the decoration.

"I won't be a hindrance," I tell her. "I won't get in the builders' way. In fact, if you think about it, they can't really do without me, because who else knows things about the house?" Like how to operate the stubborn stopcock on the water system, where the fusebox is, or what to do when the geese from the Millhouse come into the kitchen.

"But where will you sleep?" she says. And despite the fear that edges her voice, I feel the first flutter of hope, because she hasn't said "no".

"In my room," I reply. "They can do it last. It will take two weeks, three, even, for them to finish downstairs, then there are nine other bedrooms, the bathrooms – the landing alone will take days." I reel off the rooms. Twenty-three in all; twenty-five if you count the boathouse and the attic. But I don't, because the boathouse, though it will be sold as a chattel, is not part of Eden proper – not to her. It is its own land, and she wouldn't dare, has never dared, to enter.

There's the attic, too, but we don't mention that either.

"And the kitchen's done," I add, before I linger on it, before she can think of it. "Which means you don't need to worry about me starving."

Aunt Julia folds her arms as if she is cold, her polished nails pale shells against the dark of her goosepimpled cruise tan. "But there's no one to cook," she tries instead.

"I can cook. We learned at school. Beef pie and eggs en cocotte." And six other dishes that Mrs Beadle demonstrated and I obediently replicated, then immediately forgot, having no intention of cooking in the future she imagined for us as wives and mothers. But then I have no intention of cooking now; can barely eat as it is. There's cereal in the larder, bread in the freezer for toast, and an account at Cardew's in the village if I'm desperate.

"What if there's an accident?" she tries, her forehead puckering into a frown, one hand worrying the locket at her throat.

"I'll phone 999. Or Mr Garrett." The ex-Chief Constable who is everyone's Sheriff and Batman and everyday Jesus rolled into one.

"What if the electricity goes? It always goes."

"I'll row to the village."

"At night?"

"Tom's then," I lie.

She pauses and I can tell she's weakening, is already weak from the divorce, from death, from too many Tramadol. But she tries one last shot, a backhand.

"But think of what you could do in London. The galleries, the theatres... And there's that girl, from school— What's her name? Etchingham?"

"Thea Etchingham?"

"Yes. Dorothea. That's it. What about her?"

I think of Thea, with her perfect fringe and her perfect grade score; a girl who offered her friendship to me at the same glib speed with which she took it away once the Grosvenor twins saved her a place at refectory. "She's in Cannes," I say. "All summer." And the ball is returned neatly over the net.

"I don't know," she says finally. "I don't understand what's to be gained. It seems as if you're just putting off the inevitable. You'll have to come for Christmas, of course."

"Christmas is months away," I say. "And a lot of maybes." Maybe the house won't sell. Maybe I'll dig up my fortune in the damp earth and buy Eden myself. Maybe the world will end.

"You can't live on maybes," she sighs.

Bea did, I think. She lived for the maybes, the slim possibilities, the one-in-a-million chances.

I have back-ups. Plans B and C. I will chain myself to the iron gates, a suffragette for my cause, refusing food and shelter until my demand – for the cessation of time – is met. Or take our boat and row out to sea, to a far-flung isle where the sun never sets and the larder is always full.

But I don't need them. I can see by the sag of her shoulders and the set of her jaw that she is defeated. And, eventually, after a long and tedious phonecall to Uncle John, after an extracted promise that I will not get in the way of the decorators, or unpack boxes, or go unaccompanied to the pub, after a last "look-at-what-you-could-have-won" listing of the alleged pleasures of London, she gives in, and gives me my prize: a set of keys, and a last summer at Eden. With Bea.

NOVEMBER 1987

BEA SITS *at her dressing table and pushes perfume bottles, odd earrings, a half-full mug of tea aside to make room for her pad of thick cream writing paper – a present from her mother. Though it isn't Julia she's writing to, has no need to, for she saw her at the Connaught last week and their conversation barely stretched through tea and scones.*

"I thought you'd be brimming with news," said her mother, placing the paper-thin porcelain cup carefully back on its saucer.

And Bea is, but she can't tell her mother about him. She has sketched a vague outline for her, but the colour, the fine detail; that is reserved for Evie. It doesn't matter that nothing has happened – yet. It doesn't matter that Evie still hasn't written back to her last letter. That was never the point. She just wants to imagine her sat wide-eyed at the thrill of it all. The point is in the telling.

Evie, you would love him, *she begins.*

Everyone does. Bea thinks of him now, sat on the steps of the union, holding court like a robber king in his faded T-shirt and torn jeans. Money means nothing to him. It is art that matters, art and love and life itself.

James cares about art too, he knows Brecht and Büchner, has wept over Coleridge and declared he would die for love. But with him there is an edge of desperation. He is Buttons to Penn's Prince Charming with his endless clowning in class, pretending to be other players: now James Dean, now Jimmy Stewart or Laurence Olivier.

But Penn doesn't need to pretend to be anyone. He is someone. Not like James, not like the village boys, not like Tom.

She bristles at the memory. She had gone too far that time, she knew it even then as she pushed her lips against his, her bikini-clad breasts against his bare chest. It wasn't meant to hurt. It was just boredom, and cheap, tepid wine she'd hocked from the post office when Mrs Polmear was weighing out humbugs.

Or was it? For she'd known what she was doing, had needed it, her dependency as strong as an addict's for alcohol or amphetamines. She wanted to be adored. Wanted him to look at her like she knew he looked at Evie.

She feels the sharp prick of guilt, a needling in her side, but shakes it off. She's said sorry, and it's not as if Tom and Evie would ever have come to anything. She's away at school most of the time and he must be leaving for college next year, and that would be that. Besides, falling for the boy next door is so pathetically provincial, the stuff of Jackie *magazine and bad TV drama. The best ones – the Holden Caulfields and Hamlets – have lived bigger lives, better lives; have stories to tell. Stories like Penn's.*

You should see him, *she writes.* He walks through the world like it's butter and he's a hot, sharp knife. Oh! That sounds good, doesn't it! I may take up poetry after all. Become Sylvia Plath, only without the oven and dreary clothes. Penn shall be my Ted though, I'm sure of it. We haven't kissed, not yet. But we will, I'm sure of it. Besides, this is the best part, isn't it? The longing, the anticipation of it. Like a birthday party. All those balloons and games and cake, and then you unwrap the present at the end of it all and it turns out to be something you already have, or it breaks after five minutes, or you get bored. Why did I never realize that before? Remember Billy Barton? Ugh, what was I thinking? That under the fat, hairy exterior of farmer's boy he'd turn out to be some kind of soulful Byron or Shelley?

Penn's not like that. He's not like anyone I've met, and he's too full of secrets to tire of. Everyone thinks they know him but they don't, not really. They don't know he once had a pet beetle called Humbug, or that he broke his arm when he was three falling from the laundry-room window pretending to be Icarus. They think he has this perfect, gilded life with a rich, famous daddy and a place at the RSC already in the bag. They don't see that he's suffered to be here, made sacrifices, upset his family. They don't know the half of it, Evie.

She writes more. About college itself; about her halls, about the late night parties, the early rehearsal calls, the end-less, wondrous drama of it all. She mentions James, too, of course.

But it is Penn who takes up the best words. And all her thoughts.

JULY 1988

TWO DAYS later, Aunt Julia is gone. Back to the bright lights, big city in her Golf convertible, leaving behind the boxes, the house, and me.

In her place is a freezer full of ready meals and a list of instructions: who to call if the decorators don't come, or if the water pipes burst, or the coal man turns up despite being told not to bother any more. Or if wolves come from France through a secret tunnel, I think, like we feared they would, wished they would, tapping nervously, excitedly, on wooden panels along the hallway to check for hidden passages, willing it to be so. Who will protect me then? I wonder. Who will protect me, now that she cannot?

I stand idly in the kitchen, sipping water from a plastic

beaker – a pink scratched thing that reminds me of packed lunches and picnics – and picking at a box of crackers. I am still not hungry.

"Hey."

I start. The beaker of water slips out of my hand and clatters across the floor, a pool of oil-black wetness spreading across the slate.

And then I laugh, unbidden; with a relief that I have to hide as quickly as it emerged. Because it's him. Of course it's him. Who would protect me if the wolves came? Tom. Always Tom.

"As if by magic," I say.

"Ha ha." He stoops to pick up the pink plastic cup, and hands it back to me.

"It wasn't supposed to be funny," I say, taking it back delicately and dropping it on the counter.

"Then congratulations," he smiles.

But the smile fades, for the joke, the ease, feels false. Because this is not who we are any more.

I look down. The water is inching slowly, deliciously, towards my bare toes.

"You going to clear that up?" he asks.

I shrug. "It's only water."

"Jesus, Evie. You're supposed to be looking after the house."

I watch as he takes a tea towel from a plastic hook, drops it on the puddle as he drops to his knees. He is always doing the right thing, I think. Always sweeping up after people. Or trying to; their mess, their problems. Good, I would say to myself as I watched him trying in vain to coax a gull from washed-up netting. He is a good person. "A do-gooder," Bea would snort. Just not good enough for her, it turned out.

"I thought you were doing that," I say. "Keeping tabs. Isn't that why you're here?"

He looks up at me, his eyes unreadable under that lock of hair. He pushes it behind his ear once, twice. "No. I came to see if you'd changed your mind. If you wanted to stay with us after all. You know, with all the disruption."

"Is this your mum's idea?"

He pauses. "No. Mine." And I don't know if it's true. Or if I want it to be. If I want him to care, still. To be that Tom who carried me home from the pub that time, who put me to bed, who left a glass of water on the bedside table and a bucket on the floor, just in case.

But it makes no difference. It would still be the same answer.

"I can't," I say. "I just—" my voice cracks.

"Hey, it's OK." He touches my arm briefly, and I feel a shiver through me, a confusion of want and anger.

"Is it … is it because of last summer? Because we'll be fine. Me and you, I mean. We'll work it out. Work something out."

But I don't want to work anything out with Tom. Not now, maybe never. It's not about us any more; about what might have been or never could. We were nothing and we are nothing. It's about me and Bea. That's all that matters now.

I want to be here with her.

Now that Aunt Julia's gone I feel it more than ever. She's in every crack in the floorboards, every keyhole. She's in the scraps of sunlight that fracture through leaded windows, in the cool wind that whistles down the chimney at night bringing ash and bird droppings in its wake. Her hopscotch steps ring out on the flags in the scullery; her laugh is caught in the heavy drape of the drawing-room curtains. When she runs, she sends motes of dust swirling into the light, catching on my clothes, and in my hair.

She came back after all. And so I have to stay. Even in the clatter and clutter that is to come. Even with the army of strangers who will march through the halls, whistling tunelessly to tinny radio as they steam and scrape the heavy flock from the walls.

I want strangers. I want to be unknown. I want to be alone. Alone with her.

"I can't," I say. "I just … can't." And it is the truth. And he knows it.

"Well you know where I am."

"Always," I say. "As if by magic."

"Ha bloody ha." And this smile is not forced or fake. It is guileless, honest. And for a fleeting second it is how it always was. We are how we always were.

But then the smile fades, the feeling evaporates, and he is gone. And it is just me again. Me alone in Eden.

NOVEMBER 1987

BEA CONSCIOUSLY *tilts her head, twirls a lock of her hair, touching herself so that he'll think about doing the same. "Will you do me a favour?" she asks.*

Penn grins, "For you? Anything. D'you want me to fight a duel with Freddie Hatcher for your honour?"

Bea laughs, leans forward, "No. Too messy. Besides, I don't like Freddie. He's got a wart on his right hand and he reads sci-fi!"

"You're right. He stands no chance. What then? Slay a dragon? Write your Gothic paper? Or is it money?"

"No!" She's indignant now. That's not why she wants him, not like the others who borrow a tenner here, a twenty there. "It's for a friend."

"Hetty?"

"James."

"The Northern kid?"

"He's not just a 'Northern kid'." She swipes a hand half-heartedly at Penn's leg, still smiling. "He's good, you know he is. You saw his Prospero. Besides, he's a friend."

Penn pauses, a pause she knows is made up of "what is he to her?" and "what is she to him?". He is a friend, that's all. But she won't tell Penn that. Because this way works better.

"What does he need?" he asks finally.

"Nothing big. Just that he's had this dream since he was a kid. About playing Hamlet, you know. That it is him. But he won't audition against you."

"You want me to stand down?" Penn's face darkens.

"No," she says quickly. "I would never ask that. Just that if you encouraged him, maybe worked with him a bit, then he'd at least try for it."

"Aren't you going for Ophelia?"

"Of course."

"So whoever gets the part gets you."

"It's a play, dahling," she mocks. "Not real life."

But it's all intertwined here. What happens on stage spills out into the everyday. She knows James won't get the part. But she feels an urge to help him. It's odd, she has never had a need to nurture before. Or maybe only with Evie. That's what she sees in him, she thinks, suddenly. He is like Evie, he has a kind of neediness that only she seems to be able to fulfil.

"Please," she says. "Pretty please with ice cream and cherries on the top?"

Penn rolls his eyes. "Fine," he says. "You win. But don't expect me to go down without a fight."

"Never," she answers.

But as she watches them rehearse together, she realizes she was wrong. James doesn't need Penn's help. He isn't just good, he is astonishing. But if he gets the part, and she gets Ophelia, then what will happen to Penn? What will happen to the promise of them? She is Penn's Ophelia. Not James's. Isn't she?

The cast list goes up on a Friday, their fates typed out on thin foolscap. Penn is at the top, of course, always at the top. James, though, is lost among the faceless ranks of the chorus, his surname carelessly misspelt. And Bea, his Ophelia, is destined for someone else.

"He's perfect," Camilla Gordon says, sighing. "Isn't he? Perfect for the part."

James nods. For a week he had believed he stood a chance. Bea had made him believe, with her pleading and pushing him to sign up. Penn too, telling him he was made for it, born to it. Those were just lies, he understands that now, empty praise to please Bea. Praise Penn could afford to proffer because there was never any doubt about who would win in the end.

"It should have been you," she says to him later.

They're in her room. She at the dressing table, him on

her narrow bed, his back against the wall and his heart half broken, a blade stuck in.

"Hamlet, I mean. We all think it. Even Penn."

Maybe it's the truth, or maybe she is just placating him. But whichever, it doesn't change the reality of it.

"He's a third year," James shrugs. "And he'll be good. You know he will."

She looks over at him, their eyes meeting in the flyblown glass of a junk-stall mirror they chose together on East Street, as they transformed her room in a single Saturday from Barratt home to boudoir. And he flicks his hair into his face, declaims "O, what a rogue and peasant slave am I!", mimicking Penn's West London drawl, his dropped "t"s failing to disguise seven years of Eton and a lifetime of silver spoons.

"God, that's uncanny," she laughs.

But then she turns her eyes away, focusing instead on some perceived imperfection on her chin. "Pity me, then," she sighs. "I'm the one who has to kiss him."

Thirteen streets and half a mile away Penn sits at the kitchen table idly flicking a penknife open and shut. He knows it was wrong: asking Ben, the director, to drop James. But Ben owed him – for dope, for food, for the three months he'd spent sleeping on the sofa when his girlfriend kicked him out – and besides, he had to do it, had no choice. He had to get her on her own, get her away from that boy who clung to her so pathetically.

She wasn't James's to cling to, she was Penn's. She would be Penn's.

AUGUST 1988

WHEN WE were little, Bea and me, people would ask us what we wanted to be when we grew up. Bea was precise in her answers, though they changed as often as the wind from shore to sea. "An empress," she would tell our grandfather. Then, a week later to Mrs Ennor in the village: "A nurse." She worked her way through them all with the pace and clarity of a skipping rhyme: mermaid, lady, gypsy, queen. Rich man, poor man, beggar man, thief. Until she settled on one, and her answer to everyone – to her parents, to Mrs Ennor, to the girls in her dorm or the boys in the Lugger – was the same: "An actress. I'm going to be an actress." It didn't take a shrink to know that that way she could be all things at once; all heroes and villains. She could be Carol in *Road*, dressed in a mini-skirt and high heels, her vowels lengthened, her speech hardened by the broad Bolton accent; she could be light-as-air Titania, queen of the fairies; she could be Iphigenia, Eurydice, Medea. Whomever she chose, whenever she chose; a thousand futures wrapped in one.

Tom, too, changed from pirate to pilot to carpenter, before settling on lawyer.

But me? My reply never changed. I would always say, "Here."

Tom and Bea would laugh, thinking I was confused, had misunderstood or misheard the question. "Not where, *what*. *What* do you want to be?"

But I would look blank, and repeat my answer: "Here," I would say, then louder, insisting, "I just want to be here."

Because here was a whole, perfect world of wonder, limitless in its possibility, an endless new territory to be explored and charted. I wanted to stand with my back nestled in the curvature of the morning-room wall, held steadfast by its oddness and the surety of history. I wanted to roll my finger on the rounded brown Bakelite of the light switch at my bedroom door – on and off, on and off, my breath rising and falling with each satisfying click. I wanted to lie face-down in the tangled fur of the sheepskin rug on the landing, smelling its lanolin sweetness, absorbing every footfall, every figure that had passed. I wanted to hide inside my grandmother's wardrobe, our door to Narnia, a mothball-scented dressing-up box of furs and flapper dresses and long-forgotten gowns.

The house was a story, a book that caught us in time, trapped us like silverfish in a leather-bound volume of Dickens; like the dust that lay thick and heavy on the stone mantels and window sills, that caught in the folds of fabric and blew like tumbleweed across the pantry floor.

Like the damp that defied a battery of attempts to banish it. That, despite shuttered windows, and air bricks, found its way back in; oozing through every fault and fissure, sending wet fingers along the scullery floor, into the brocaded seams of wing-backed chairs and into the highest shelves and bottom drawers of cupboards, rendering biscuits and breakfast cereals a claggy, stale mass.

But it was this damp air that fed our fertile imaginations, curious thoughts growing like pin mould on pantry bread. The house became our Neverland – full of strange creatures and terrible monsters and magic, magic everywhere. But now this land of make-believe was being dismantled, piece by rotting piece. That sweet, musty smell – of the past, of a hundred lives and a thousand stories – was replaced by eye-stinging sawdust and the bitter, chemical tang of gloss paint. And the peace that hung over Eden like a sacred shroud was driven out, shooed across the lawns by the high-pitched, angry buzz of electric drills and sanders.

A week later, I follow it; slip from the back of the wardrobe and, taking an apple, a sandwich and a paperback book, I slide out the back door and into the woods.

* * *

The path to the boathouse is narrow now. Spindly nettles nod and waver a warning towards my bare calves as I pass, and the once well-trodden soil is overgrown. Brambles whip my thighs, thin scratches of red against pale skin. Yet I run on regardless, my plimsolls skimming over clods of earth and the exposed roots of oaks, beeches, and the last of the elms. I fly, second star to the right and straight on until I reach my morning: a wide curve of water that glistens in the early sun – Calenick creek – and next to it, a faded-board boathouse, with a corrugated roof and painted "No Entry" tacked haphazardly, childishly, across the door.

If Eden was our world, then the boathouse was our playroom: a ready-made gingerbread house in an enchanted forest, picture-book perfect with red-checked curtains, a table and chairs, a camping stove. We would spend all day here, playing at pirates, at Swallows and Amazons, at Charon ferrying the dead across the Styx, taking turns to row our boat – *Jorion* – across to the Millhouse and back, Tom paying us for the journey in penny chews or strawberry bootlaces. We would swim out to the pontoon, lie on our backs until our skin stung from salt and sunshine, until our throats were hoarse from singing that Robert de Niro was waiting; until, when we pressed against our eyelids, shooting stars danced across the pinkness like fireworks on New Year's Eve. Then, at night, when we dared, we would sleep top to tail in the foldaway camp bed or on the floor, waking with toes in our faces and the world upside-down to a breakfast of biscuits and cherryade.

And then one summer Bea just stopped coming. At first there was a film she wanted to see at the Lux in Liskeard; an American high school thing of rebellion and leather jackets and boys from the wrong side of the tracks. Then the excuses rolled off her tongue as easily as marbles: too many goodbyes to be said to schoolfriends; too many shopping trips to Plymouth for pillows and sheets and shoes; too many scripts to be read in the solitude of the attic, where my splashing couldn't soak the pages, and my sulking couldn't distract her study.

And oh how I sulked. I sulked with the same determination with which she ignored me. Because I couldn't play alone any more. I was a cowboy with no Indian, a Wendy with no Pan. I would sit in my own room and curse, pray for a plague of locusts or frogs, make pacts with shadowy figures I conjured up in my own netherworld of self-pity. Until I was forced to admit our days of Hansel and Gretel were over. And that's when I turned to Tom. He became my partner in crime, my faithful sidekick, and I his. Though I hoped, prayed, I would be more. Then one night we rowed back late from the village and collapsed side by side in the boathouse, too heavy-limbed and lazy to make it any further than the creek.

Even now I still feel the heft of the boards beneath my back, the sheet clinging to my sweat-sticky body, the perfect proximity of him.

"Are you awake, Evie?" he said.

"No," I replied.

He laughed, then. "Me neither."

"I'm hot," I said, cursing myself for stating the obvious. For not being able to articulate what I really wanted to tell him.

"I'm hot, too," he echoed.

And then it happened. He went first: stripped off his T-shirt and shorts. And though it was dark, and he was no more than a silhouette, a shadow, I knew he was naked. And, though I'd seen him like that so many times before as children, this, this was different. This meant something else.

"Your turn," he said.

And, with the sound of my heart pounding in my chest, and his breath quickening, I peeled off my clothes until only my white knickers remained in their pathetic, virginal glory. They should be black, I remember thinking, or lacy. I should have borrowed some of Bea's.

But Tom didn't notice. Or didn't care. Because then, there, on the floor of the boathouse, the same floor we'd played Peter Pan on, played pirates on, he kissed me.

The rest is a jumble of images – ones I have had to imagine, conjure from the darkness that shrouded us: my hands on his chest, his back; his moving down my legs, then up again; my knickers pulled aside. Then my hand pushing his away, panic slowly taking hold: that I can't do this. That I'm not like Bea. I'm not Bea.

"It's OK," he says. "It's fine."

But it isn't.

We lay in silence until sleep took him, and then, before the clock struck twelve, I ran away from the shame of it. Not of what happened, but what didn't. That I couldn't go through with it after all. That I was the child he always thought of me as.

I awoke the next day to an afternoon so blistering I had no choice but to swim. I will tell him, I thought, as I pulled on my bathing suit. I will tell him that I'm sorry, that I love him, that I do want him, I do. And he will understand. Of course he will.

So convinced was I of the absolute truth of this that I didn't think to wonder whether he wanted me too.

But then I heard it, that laughter, a peal of applause scattering through the trees, then his, lower, wine-sodden, then silence. A silence that urged me on as strongly as it told me to go back. Because when I emerged from the woods to seek its source, I saw it was a silence borne of a kiss.

That was the last time either of us came here.

I slide the rusting lock from its housing, and step from a world where everything is in flux into one in which nothing has changed.

For there is the table and chairs. There are the red-checked curtains; the gingham faded now in the sun, but still bright, still sending out its cheery welcome. The camp bed unfolded, waiting for weary occupants, its rickety legs bowed on one side from where Bea tried to use it as a trampoline.

My chest tightens, and I feel the strange fullness and emptiness of it all; of a world suspended in aspic, and yet in the centre of it all is a Bea-shaped hole, so that at any minute this precarious construction might collapse in on itself.

I have made a terrible mistake staying here. I should have gone to London with Aunt Julia. I will call her, I think, and go on the next train.

But as I turn to go, I see a rucksack in the corner, leaning against the wall, a dull green against dirty whitewash. The kind you get from army surplus. Bea and I customized ours with swirling felt-tip paisley patterns and pin badges of bands. But this one has no pen marks. No badges. There is no clue as to who owns this bag. It is clean and new and unspoilt.

All I know is that whoever left it must be coming back.

DECEMBER 1987

TERM IS *almost over and Hamlet has closed its run, a success. James is praised for his part, but Bea and Penn are a "triumph", their chemistry "undeniable".*

This crackling, electric thing between her and Penn has taken Bea by surprise. Though she willed it, hoped it. It had been there when rehearsals had started. In every word spoken, every choreographed glance, touch. She was afraid it would be lost when they had to kiss. That somehow the stark practice room, the strip lights, the stares from Ben, from James and the stage hands, would drive it away. But even on a wet afternoon, surrounded by everyone, with the sounds of traffic on the Lewisham Road and the smell of coffee and someone's stale crisps, she had felt something, everything; she had felt as if she had touched his very soul, and he hers.

They had repeated the kiss later, in her room, under the pretext of another run-through.

"That wasn't a rehearsal," he said, when he finally pulled away. "Not for me."

Bea couldn't speak, just shook her head and pulled him back to her.

It wasn't until later, when they were lying next to each other in the narrow space of a single bed, that she found the words. "I knew it would be like this," she whispered. "Didn't you? Didn't you just know it?"

He nods, pushes a strand of damp hair back from her face. "I've wanted you for ever. Since the first time I saw you."

Bea feels a rush of relief that she was right all along. That love could feel like this. For the first time she has done something right. She can stop searching now.

"We won't tell anyone at college, though," she insists. "Not yet."

"But— Why not?"

"I— It's not that I don't want to. I want to tell the world, believe me. They should know how good this is. Just— I need to let them – him – down gently."

For a moment she thinks Penn is angry, is going to insist. But he doesn't. Of course he doesn't, she tells herself. He understands her and her odd feelings for this strange boy. "Whatever you want," he says. "Whenever you're ready."

"After the show," she thinks aloud. "We can tell people after the show."

* * *

*James watches them – Queen Bea and King Penn – being
carried by their adoring crowd to the palace on Telegraph
Hill, and he one of the throng. He has watched them like
this for weeks, worrying, suspecting, that something has been
finalized between them but never finding anything concrete.
She has been vague in her answers, changing the subject and
imploring him not to "talk shop" all the time.*

*"I tell you everything about me," he announces one even-
ing. "Did you know that?"*

But she doesn't rise to it. Just says, "I'm glad."

*He tries another tactic. "Gina Seaton tried to kiss me in
the green room."*

*"Really?" The disbelief she fails to hide hurts him. As if
she cannot imagine anyone wanting him that way.*

"Really," he repeats. "I said no."

*"Well, you're a fool," she replies finally. "She's got fantastic
tits."*

*And now they are here, all three of them. In a house
bought for Penn by his father; an investment, for everything
comes down to money. His parents will do it up once Penn
is gone and sell it for a fortune. But for now, the decaying
Victorian terrace has gained a kind of notoriety on campus,
its tenants the most daring, its parties the most decadent, its
drug supply guaranteed by a man called Sugar Slim. The
house is their palace and their playground.*

*Only James sees it for what it is: nothing but a larger
version of the back-to-backs at home on Hornby Road. The*

swirled nylon carpets in psychedelic brown and orange and yards of cheap anagylpta to cover the cracks in the walls are a reminder of everything he left behind. He feels needling shame as he recognizes a fake Canaletto as the same gaudy print that hangs above the mantel at his Aunty Maureen's semi.

He climbs the staircase, stepping over bodies in this cut-price Bruegel or Hogarth. Their heads bowed, they strain to hear each other over Mick Jagger's swagger as they regurgitate theories from student papers and bar-room politics, concepts they cannot truly understand – not like he and Bea. They are cuckoos, hermit crabs, inhabiting the lives of the working class as if they were their own, as if the fight was theirs to battle. Yet he, he is different. His was an accident of birth: the wrong place, the wrong parents. Parent. He is destined to a life with better lighting, and wine from well-stocked cellars, not pound-a-bottle Bulgarian vinegar from Anil at the Minimart.

He can't stand to listen any longer, so he pushes open the nearest door, looking for escape, but finds instead that he has walked into the lion's den.

They're against the wall: his broad, rugby-built back covering her body so that it is her hand that James recognizes first, the turquoise and silver of her ring glinting as she pulls his head to hers. Penn pushes into her body, and her foot falters, shifting her into view. And even though Bea's eyes are closed, James imagines that he sees in them want, lust, love.

Feelings he has waited so long to see in her face, and now they are not for him.

But for Penn.

He closes the door silently, walks back down the stairs, out of this pleasure-dome, and back to his own small, stark reality.

The flat is above a kebab shop on the Old Kent Road, a single room that seems to heave with furniture – a bed that doubles as a sofa; a desk; an easy chair, its springs collapsed and jutting through the nap-worn fabric. There's no kitchen – instead a stove and sink have been forced uncomfortably under the grimy sash window, so that when he boils an egg or cleans his teeth he looks out on a vista of industrial bins and, beyond, the slow, painful procession of Folkestone-bound lorries.

The bathroom is down a strip-lit corridor – a single shower and toilet he shares with a Geordie bricklayer and three generations from Nigeria, so that more than once he's had no choice but to urinate in his own sink, or out of the window into the yard below. And the smell. Cheap meat and chip fat clings to every surface in a thin patina of grease, so that even the clothes pushed to the back of the cupboard that stands for a wardrobe carry the same stale odour as the workers downstairs.

He could have gone into halls – the big new-build blocks up near Deptford with bright walls, clean carpets and an en suite. Could have had two meals a day cooked for him, and a cleaner once a week. But then he'd be one of them with their cheques from daddy and their shiny new complete sets of Shakespeare and their identikit posters – Betty Blue, The Wall, Che. He would have been no better than his da, doing what's expected of him. Those kids in halls reminded him of sheep, or, worse, rats. Whereas, living like this, he is the Pied Piper.

So he found the rooms in Loot. £140 a month inc. bills, no DSS, Old Kent Road – a Monopoly address, the brown-topped back alley his sisters dismissed so airily, holding out for the glamour of Mayfair or Pall Mall. A road he, too, once balked at as a child playing the game on Boxing Day. But his ma laughed and said, "It's London. Doesn't matter where you are in London, Seamus, all of the streets there are paved with gold."

And while he is yet to see a gilded glimmer amongst the dog shit and spit and discarded cans that litter the pavement outside, it is cheap, it is close to college, and most of all, it is his and his alone.

And Bea's, one day, he had hoped.

But now, as he sits at the window, bathed in the sour acid orange of streetlights, he realizes what a fool he has been. He can't compete with Penn. Not in terms of tangible, touchable things.

He needs an edge. He needs words or deeds that will out-shine even a king. Or a secret that only he can tell. And he smiles into the night sky, for now he has renewed purpose. He will give Bea things Penn cannot: experiences, places, feel-ings. He will show her he is not just worthy, but that he is the better man.

He doesn't know how, or when, or what yet. Just that he will.

AUGUST 1988

I CROUCH down, my fingers shaking as I try to unlatch the webbing, fumbling over the cold metal of the buckle. But then it's done, and as I pull back the flap I feel myself hold my breath, as if I'm Jim Hawkins knelt at a treasure chest, about to find gold bullion, or a gun.

But it's neither. No bright glint of florins, no hard iron of a barrel, just the soft, dull cloth of T-shirts and trousers and the broken spines of books. I pull out copies of *On The Road*, a Wesker Trilogy, *Hamlet*, the stuff of A-level set texts, or the idle dreams of a wannabe Holden Caulfield. I feel like Hayley Mills in that black and white film where she thinks she's found Jesus in her barn, and he turns out to be nothing but a common thief, a criminal. Only he, whoever he is, does not even seem to be that.

I push the books back down into the bag and go to relatch the buckle when I see an envelope sticking out from one of the side pockets. Its fatness beckons me and I pull it out, like a rabbit from a hat.

And then I start. For there is money, lots of it – wads of it. Not the neat kind you see in gangster films, fresh from a bank, but different notes, a jumble of browns and purples and reds. But it's not that that's jolted me. It's the address on the front that stops me in my tracks, that sends my stomach to my mouth and tremors to my feet: Will Pennington, 73 Pepys Road, Telegraph Hill, London.

There's a sound behind me, the creak of a deckboard swollen with saltwater and dried in the sun. "As if by magic" I think. But when I turn, it's not Tom I see. It's another boy. Thinner, slighter. His face in shadow, he's framed in the doorway, light haloing out behind him like the archangel Gabriel so that, for a second, I think I can see his wings. Then he steps forward, his face clear now, pale, as if he's seen a ghost. Maybe he has, for he says a single word, and I feel the ground give way beneath me and darkness descend.

Because what he says is, "Bea?"

APRIL 1988

SHE SLIPS *into the role of Penn's girlfriend with the same elegant ease that she becomes Ophelia, Viola, Blanche Du-Bois. She moulds herself to the shape of his world – the late nights running to early mornings, the parties, the plans for post-graduation: an experimental piece at a festival in Venice. He tells her about his father – about his dark moods, and the dark clouds that have appeared on his lungs edging out the anger and replacing it with a fear that makes him clutch at his family for the first time.*

"It's sad, really. Pathetic," he says.

"What is?"

"That it takes disease to cure him."

"You think he's cured?"

"Of being a complete bastard? For the moment. Until…"
Penn trails off, disappears into himself.

She holds him then, tighter, closer than she has ever held
him before and whispers to him that she understands what it
means to feel a father's disappointment. Their bitterness at
you and at what you might become radiates from them – a
seamless aura of imagined loss.

Penn takes her to meet him, at the Commons, for he still
goes to work, despite this thing that grows like mould inside
him. They walk hand in hand behind him down the green-
carpeted corridors for tea on the terrace above the grey-brown
waters of the Thames.

"So what do your parents do?" his father asks her.

"My father's a midget strongman in the circus," she dead-
pans. "And my mother was a charwoman."

Penn kicks her under the table and she fails to stifle a laugh.

But the old man smiles, lets himself be the butt of the joke
and Penn squeezes her hand and she knows she's done the right
thing. She is proud and pleased that being Bea is the right thing.

Later she tells Penn of the river at home, the creek,
how different its greenness, its wooded banks are to this vast
muddy thing called the Thames. She tells him she'll take him
there one day, to Eden.

"You can meet everyone," she promises. "There's this old
woman at the Post Office – Mrs Polmear – she's like a walking gossip column. And the Rapsey twins – Joyce and Edna.
Can you imagine still living with your sister when you're in
your fifties?"

Penn shrugs and Bea remembers with shame that, like her, he is an only child. But unlike her, he doesn't have an Evie.

"You'll like her," she says. "She's like me."

"Is she strange, then?" he laughs and pulls her to him.

"Yes, very," she laughs.

"Does she look like you?" He traces his finger down her collarbone, pushes his hand into her bra to feel her breast.

"A bit," she breathes.

"Does she kiss like you?"

But Bea doesn't answer, for his mouth is on hers, his hands are on her. Evie is forgotten, drowned out in the surge of their desperation, their need and the swell of The Smiths on his new CD player singing, "There is a Light".

By Easter she's given up her room in halls and moved the flyblown mirror into the house on Telegraph Hill, her beaded dresses hung about the walls like bright butterflies pinned and mounted on paper.

And James watches it all, a spectator at a vital match as Penn and Bea's lives take centre stage, and his own is pushed further into the wings. Bea misses lunches with him, leaves notes pinned to the board to tell him she can't run lines because she's going to the country for the weekend.

"You're disappearing," he tells her. "He's taking you all for himself."

But she laughs it off. "He doesn't own me. He doesn't tell me what to do."

No one tells Bea what to do, least of all him. So he tries another tactic.

"I miss you," he admits. "I miss how we used to be."

"I miss you too," she says. "We'll see each other, I promise. It's just … it's hard right now, with his dad and everything. He needs me."

I need you, he thinks. And as he looks into her eyes, he knows she needs him too. He just has to wait.

AUGUST 1988

WHEN I open my eyes he hasn't flown away on his feathered wings. Yet I've moved: I'm out on the deck now. He must have carried me here for air, and light.

I can see him more clearly now. There's no halo, of course not. Just a tangled mop of hair. And in place of an angel's robe he's wearing a faded T-shirt and tight black jeans. He's not an angel. Yet he's not from this world either, or he'd be in deck shoes and chinos like the weekenders, or work clothes like the village boys.

I sit up, my head dizzy from the fall, from the fright. "Penn," I say. "You're Penn."

He frowns. "Who are you?"

"Evangeline," I say. "Evie."

"Not Bea," he says. "God, of course not." He looks away then, as if he's fighting back tears, or anger, or disappointment.

"No." I am nobody. I am the not-Bea, the wannaBea. The never-will-Bea.

But yet, to him, I am somebody. Somebody he has heard of, at least.

"Her cousin," he says, remembering.

I nod, my own face frowning now.

"You weren't at her funeral," I say.

"I—"

"Your father," I blurt. "I'm sorry. I didn't mean… He – he died?" I say pointlessly.

"Y–yes. He died. I couldn't come then. I'm— I'm so sorry. I—"

"It's OK," I interrupt quickly.

His accent is rootless. Not the braying drawl I imagined it would be.

"You came now," I say. Like he said he would in his letter. He came anyway.

"Yes, I— I hitched."

"She hitched all the time," I say. "To Calenick. To Plymouth even."

But he'll know this. He won't want to hear it now and be reminded of her. I fall silent again.

"What? What is it?"

"Nothing," I say. I hug my arms around my legs. It is hot, yet I am shivering, my skin dappled with goosebumps.

"She's gone," I say. "Aunt Julia – Bea's mum, I mean. If that's who you came to see," I add.

"It's not who I came to see."

Then who? Why come? To see Eden? To see *me*? I push the last thought away as I feel my face redden. He was Bea's. I peek a sideways glance at him – at this last piece of her, and then I realize why he's here. He doesn't want Eden or me. He wants to see Bea. Or rather traces of her, particles of her. He wants to piece them together so he can know all of her, remember everything.

Just as I do.

He reaches a hand out to me. I take it; let him pull me up. "I'm sorry I scared you," he says. And he smiles. And I see what Bea saw. That he has strength and grace and beauty. And secrets. Bea loved secrets.

I let his hand drop then, awkward again, shove mine into my pocket. "Me too," I reply. Because I know that for a split second, in the shadow of the boathouse, with his body blocking the sun, he thought I was her. He thought I was a kind of resurrection, a ghost, a double.

"I should go," he says. "This was a mistake. I—"

And I feel another sudden lurch of fear at the loss of him so quickly. "Stay," I say, the word pushing past my lips, blurting out before I can trap it under my tongue.

"What?"

"I mean it," I say. "Stay. For a bit. If you want."

"I want," he replies.

And I feel the heaviness seep out of me, I am light as

air, as gossamer. "You can sleep here in the boathouse," I say, words falling over themselves now. "We used to. And there's running water. A stove, look. And I can get you stuff. Food and things. From the house."

He nods as he watches me whirl around him. I am dancing with determination, and desperation and delight. But then he catches me, stops me mid-turn.

"Don't tell anyone," he says. "About me, I mean."

"But why?"

"I— I just don't want them talking... I mean I don't want to talk to other people. My father— I shouldn't even be here. If I'm going to stay, let's keep it a secret. Just ... just between you and me."

I feel heat in my face again. He wants to talk to me. He wants to know me. And in that second I understand. We can make it better for each other. I am all that is left of her for him and he is all that is left of her for me. We both feel guilty. We both argued with her.

"I won't tell," I say. "Promise. Wait here. I won't be long."

And I am flying again, up the path to Eden. And I feel it, I feel how I used to feel with Bea at the beginning of summer. On the brink of something; an adventure.

An awfully big adventure.

MAY 1988

THE CROWD *heaves in one violent surge to the stage, and James and Bea are carried on the wave, their cheers lost in the sound of fiddles and a drunken drum roll.*

He saved weeks for this gig – two tickets to the Pogues at the Town and Country Club. His grant money set aside in an old tobacco tin, he's been living instead on baked beans and end-of-night chips blagged from Nihal downstairs; spent his evenings soaking up the free heat of the library to avoid putting another 50p in the meter.

It was worth it though, because now he's here, with her, in the crush of bodies, and the smell of sweat, smoke and cheap alcohol.

She pulls him to her and they reel to the sound of "Sally

MacLennane". Their arms linked, he spins her around. She is a bright star in orbit and he is at the centre of her universe. This is all he wants, all he's ever wanted. And it is here and it is now. Thanks to his tickets, and her guilt.

The crowd washes stagewards and another jigging couple – a pair of beery Belfast boys – knocks into them, pushing her into his arms and crushing her against his chest. He looks down in panic, but she is laughing, intoxicated by the raw thrill of it, and delight rises again in him too.

"It's you and me against the world," he shouts.

"We're Bonnie and Clyde," she laughs, "Superman and Lois Lane."

And he is Superman. He feels it inside him tonight; mercurial, unstoppable. He pulls her face to his and kisses her hard, pushing his fire into her.

But she jerks her head away. "Just don't... Don't spoil it. OK?"

"I'm sorry. I thought—"

"Dance with me," she pleads. "I want to dance."

And she does. He watches as she spins on the arm of a stranger, his bright star disappearing into the crowd, out of his orbit.

Bea is still spinning as she gets into bed beside Penn three hours later, giddy with the thrill of beer and dancing, and ... James. She pushes the thought from her mind, along with the vestige of the girl she used to be. That girl – the one who just wanted to be wanted, who let all the boys kiss her just for the satisfaction of knowing that for those few minutes she was the centre of their world – is gone, has to be. For now she has everything she has wanted: this new life, this new love, real love. She won't ruin it.

She curls her still-clothed body round Penn's sleeping form, feels him stir and waken.

"Bea?" he asks.

"Yes," she murmurs. "It's me."

It's me and you. We are Bonnie and Clyde, she thinks. Not me and James. Me and you.

AUGUST 1988

THE CREEK is an ever-moving thing, bringing endless possibility on its slow, brown tide. In the winter it's swollen with rains and snow, taking with it a wash of china clay from the docks upriver. In the summer, the surge of seawater carries tin cans and crisp packets, the chewed balsa wood of lolly sticks; detritus from other lives. More than once it has borne a body, bloated and blue, its swollen limbs catching on the banks.

But today it has brought something else. Someone else. He is flotsam washed up by the water – not a Coke can or the torn, faded wrapper of a Cornetto, but real treasure; a pirate's chest, a message in a bottle. A piece of Bea. He has been sent to me. And so I must do all I can to keep him. So

I pack anything and everything, guessing at what he likes and what he'll need: a fruit cake from the larder; plastic bottles to collect water from the holy well; new batteries for the cassette player; a toothbrush and paste; a copy of *The Tempest*, its margins a scrawl of O-level notes and doodles of sea creatures; a tin of humbugs, striped like bees; half a bottle of French brandy kept in the larder for Crêpes Suzette, its dark amber diluted by the tea Bea added to hide her late night swigs; my sleeping bag, still fusty with the grass and dust of last summer. I pack for a single sleepover and for a month of Sundays. There's so much I want to give him. By the time I get to the back door, I'm laden with goods, like a packhorse. I have had to leave behind a box of chocolates tied up in a scarlet ribbon, a jar of preserved peaches, a book of poems, its illustrations edged in gilt. No matter. I can come back for them later. There will be tomorrow. Please let there be tomorrow.

I stumble down the step, like a smuggler carrying contraband, and a heavy secret. The sleeping bag knocks against my thigh and the mints rattle inside their tin, like a hive of sweet insects. I am so lost in the story of it all that I have forgotten to listen out for the tick-tock of the crocodile.

"Woah!"

I yelp in shock and feel the worn rubber of my shoe slip on the gravel. Then two hands grasp my arms as I pitch forward. I don't have to look up to know who it is. I can feel it in the callouses of his fingers, in the surety of his grip: Tom.

"I'm fine." I shrug his arms away and right the pack on my bag.

"Are you running away?" he asks.

"Yes," I lie. To Neverland, I think.

"Can I come?"

I panic, blurt out a staccato "No". Then I panic again at this betrayal of my secret – Penn's secret. "I— I'm just going to the creek. On my own." I add. "I need to be alone."

He nods, understanding. "Well, I'm glad you're out."

I change the subject. "I thought you'd gone to Liskeard."

"I did," he smiles. "But the market's over," he says. "It's gone one."

"Really?" Have I been at the house for over an hour? I feel panic rise in me, a swarming in my fingers and toes willing me to move, to run.

"Why? What's the hurry?"

"Nothing," I say quickly. "Just, time flies and all that."

"When you're having fun?"

I stare at him, incredulous. "This isn't about 'fun'. This is so far from fun."

This is about something else, something more. It's about death, and life – keeping Bea alive. Penn has memories of Bea I must dig out, gather up like cowrie shells or sea glass. For my own are clouded with time and dust now, and distorted by cruel words and selfishness. Whereas Penn's, Penn's will be clean, true, new. He can tell me new thoughts, new hopes, new fears. He can explain why she was coming, and why she never arrived. Maybe, maybe.

"I— I'm sorry. I didn't mean that." His hand covers his mouth as if to keep him from saying anything else.

But it's me who's gone too far. I don't want him worrying about me, following me.

"No, I'm sorry," I say. "It's just…"

"It's OK," he says. "I understand. More than you think."

He's going to say he feels the way I feel. He's going to say he loved her too. But I don't want to hear it. Not now. I don't have time to listen, or think about what that word does or doesn't mean. I need to get back to Penn, before he changes his mind. Before I lose him too.

"I have to go. Before the tide goes out," I add. "I want to swim."

"Sure," he shrugs. "But … if you need me … I mean, if you need something, anything. You know where I am."

I nod. "Thanks," I murmur. "I'll see you soon," I promise.

"Sure," he mumbles.

And I am gone. Stumbling, running, as fast as I can. As fast as I dare with my precious cargo strapped to my back. "Please be there, please be there," I repeat to myself as each footstep hits the earth. "Please be there." Until at last I burst out of the enchanted forest, a desperate, drunken Tinkerbell staggering into the bright lotus-land of the creek.

The deck is deserted, the boathouse silent now, empty. I swing round, desperately scanning the horizon. For what? For a boat sailing into the sunset? But the sun is high in the sky, and I don't even know if he can row. I feel dizzy again, my legs trembling from the run, from the weight, from the disappointment. And then I hear it.

"Evie," a voice says. "Evie. I'm here."

And I look, not out to the sea, but back into the inky green stillness of the creek. And I see him. Waist-deep in the water and half naked. Not the strong, oat-fed boy I imagined, but fragile, his skin paler. As if he is half ghost, half boy. But he is beautiful.

And he is Bea's.

I feel heat flush my cheeks with embarrassment. And I look away as he wades out of the water and takes the towel I have brought.

"Thanks." As he wraps it round his waist, I catch a glimpse of his shorts. Faded blue, like school swimming trunks. And I hate myself for liking him even more, for feeling what Bea must have felt; that he doesn't swagger or show off, that he wouldn't wear Ralph Lauren board shorts to prove he is someone.

"I brought you stuff," I say quickly.

"So I see," he smiles. Then adds, "Thanks." As if he might have seemed ungrateful. As if he, too, is trying to please.

I'm awkward in his presence; a schoolgirl again, for that is what I am, I remember. I'm not the dazzling bright drama student that Bea is – was. I'm chalk dust and knee-length socks and a box-pleat pinafore.

"Here," I say, and I rummage again in my bag then hand him my treasure. He nods and hands me a gift in return. It's a cassette, not a shop-bought one, but home-made, a mixtape.

The radio-cassette is old, its plastic back warped, the casing rusted. And so I say a silent prayer as I push the new batteries in and press play.

At first there's just the buzz of static: white noise crackling off the walls and fizzling into the ceiling. But then I hear the sudden striking of piano keys, the murmur and swell of a jeering, cheering crowd that pushes the air from me as a memory is dragged to the surface. I know this. Bea used to play it – a song that drifted down the stairs, or filled the kitchen with its defiant noise until Aunt Julia could no longer stand its minor chords and morose lyrics and would switch the player back to Radio 4 and *The Archers*.

"Last Night I Dreamt…" I say.

He smiles, finishes the title for me. "…That Somebody Loved Me."

I nod. The Smiths. God, Bea and I loved the Smiths.

"I saw them," he says. "You know, live."

"Really?" I am childishly excited. I have never been to a gig, to a disco even.

"Twice, actually," he says. "April the fourth at the Palace. Then the Free Trade Hall, October the thirtieth. Two different years though," he adds, as if he must lessen this display of devotion.

"You went all the way to Manchester? Twice?"

He is silent for a second, stares at me as if I am the strange one for not going.

"It's not that far," he says finally. "Not really."

"No," I say, anxious not to be the odd one out, to be back in the triangle that is Penn, Bea and me.

The song changes then, to the slow, mournful sound of a woman's voice. It is a lament in song and I recognize it from another tape that Bea made; one that I played again and again until it stretched and snapped and no amount of Sellotape could fix it.

It's "Song To the Siren" and I listen – we listen – as Elizabeth Fraser's voice soars and sinks as she sits on the rocks in our imagination, mermaid-like in our heads, and mourns a love lost.

"I— we used to…" But I trail off.

He takes my hand and I start at his touch; at the intimacy and yet the normalcy of it. And I feel a sudden jolt of fear at my want for this boy. My need for him.

Though maybe it's not him I want. Maybe it's what we share.

For we do share something. We share Bea. She has tied us together, and I don't want to loosen those ties, not yet. I want them tighter. I want to be bound to him so that I can feel her again. And so I let him hold me, I don't let go. I won't let go.

MAY 1988

BEA STANDS *on the lowest of the three high boards; her feet over the tip, her arms wide in worship, the people below her – her congregation – as small as ants. She has done this before, here at the lido this summer, and before at the point at Eden. She's not scared, she's invincible, beautiful Bea, and for just a few seconds of serendipitous perfection, she can fly.*

She slinks, slick with water and shining with satisfaction, back to her towel and to Penn.

"Your go," she smiles.

"Maybe later," he says.

But he won't. Not later, not today, not ever.

Bea rolls her eyes. "You're like Evie," she says.

"Evie?"

"You know, my cousin. I told you about her?"

He nods, remembering.

"She swears she wants do it, climbs to the top of the point, and then has to climb all the way down again."

"I'm not scared," he says.

But he is.

He can swim. His father made sure of that; ignored his pleas and protestations and made him jump from the side of a yacht at La Napoule. "In at the deep end," he said. "Best way to learn." And learn Penn did. But he's never managed to conquer his fear of heights, despite numerous trips up light-houses and church towers and being forced to climb ladders. However many times he tried, he'd end up stuck, with his father raging at him from below as Penn, bilious and weak, clung to walls or rungs as if they were life itself.

"How awful," she had said to him.

"I'll get over it," he had shrugged.

But he hadn't. Not yet.

"I'm sorry," Bea says. "We shouldn't have come." For his father is struggling now, his determined clutch at life weak-ening, despite the chemotherapy and special diets and private room.

"No, it's good," Penn assures her. "Good to be out." And he pulls her to him to kiss her.

"I'll do it," says James, jumping to his feet.

He can't believe he's been handed this chance, this golden opportunity. He hadn't even been going to join them.

"We're going to the lido," she'd said. "Come with us."

"I should work," he'd lied. Because he knew it was an afterthought, an invitation extended through guilt not desire.

But she'd pouted and pleaded. "You don't even have to get in. You can read a book and lounge like a lizard. Like the lizard king!"

He'd shrugged.

"Pretty please? With whipped cream, and hundreds and thousands, and a cherry on the top?"

And it worked, just like they both knew it would.

"OK, OK. Fine," he'd conceded.

She'd laughed and linked her arm through his. "You'll love it, you'll see. It's perfect."

And it almost is. There are wooden cubicles in fifties ice-cream colours, and jewel-bright bikinis on bodies that are browned, lithe. A world away from the municipal baths on Park Road, with the yellow verruca bath, the clogs of hair that tangle around your fingers and toes, the pasty-faced Donnas and Debbies, their black regulation suits straining to contain their pale, potato-fed bodies.

But every time he looks at her and sees her hands slick with Hawaiian Tropic as they glide over Penn's already tan skin, a tight, hard ball of envy establishes itself in his gut again. What is it she sees in him? In this idle rich boy, this fool who won't even dive from a board? He's not brave, he's not magnificent, he's just hair and teeth and a lazy laugh.

James has to show her what she's overlooked, what she's missing. And so, when Penn refuses to jump, he seizes his moment and pulls himself up, no longer caring that his trunks *are a size too large and a decade too old; that his skin still carries the blueish tinge of too many Lancashire winters; that his swimming is amateurish.*

He walks past the springboard – that is for pratfalls and prats like Penn. Not even Penn. Instead he heads to the high boards, climbs to the tallest of the three. And then he stands on the edge of the still-dry concrete, his arms wide like wings, like Bea's, his toes already in nothingness.

He hears their voices, faint below him.

"Jesus, what's he doing?" says someone.

"Jump!" yells a girl.

"What?" Bea turns to her, anger in her sharp movement.

"It's safe," the girl protests. "Or they wouldn't have it. No one would use it."

"No one does use it."

But he does. He will. Because he's not afraid. He's on fire, he's Icarus reaching for the sun. And so he steps off the platform and into the crackling air.

And then he's flying, swiftly, swiftly, and it's a feeling of such purity and exhilaration that there's no fear when he plunges into the water, just the knowing that he is alive.

He surfaces and then half swims, half scrabbles for the side. She's crouching there, her face etched with the surprise. It is the shock he had hoped for.

"Are you OK?"

"Course."

She laughs: a sound of undisguised relief. "You scared me."

And it's his turn to laugh. "Good," he says, and pulls himself up onto the paving slabs.

"Where are you going?"

"Again." he says. "I'm going again."

And he does. He jumps again, and again, and the others clap and cheer every leap and plunge.

All except for Penn.

Penn is riven with envy. He is losing her, he thinks. He is losing his touch. This thing with his dad is distracting him. He needs to get back in the game, though. No, not a game. This time it's real. She loves him. She tells him so again and again. And he loves her, he does. He could have had countless others: Anna, Jules, Stella. He could have Stella whenever he wanted. But he doesn't want them. He wants her. It's always been her.

But as he turns onto his stomach so he doesn't have to witness this circus, this charade, he realizes there's a scene he's never played before, has never even considered: What if she doesn't want him? What if it's James she wants after all?

AUGUST 1988

EACH MORNING I do the same: I pack hunks of bread, cheese, bottles of lemonade kept in the freezer to fend off the increasing heat, then run through the still-waking woods down to the creek to find him.

Each morning I feel the same: the blankness when I open my eyes, then the strange nausea in my stomach when I remember – the loss of her, the gain of him; the panic when I see the corrugated roof of the boathouse – that it will be empty again, he will be gone; the same relief, elation even when I see him – the tangle of his hair, his sleep-heavy eyes, the slightness of his smile.

Then one morning I'm bold enough, desperate enough to ask the question. I hug my knees, look at him sideways, affecting a kind of nonchalance that I am not feeling, that I never feel with him. "How much longer are you staying?" I say.

"You want me to go?" he asks, his eyes clouded by hurt.

"No, no," I say quickly. "I want you to stay— I mean, you can stay. If you want," I add.

"Then I'll stay," he says, finally. "For a bit."

And I will take that "a bit". For a bit is longer than a day. Maybe even a summer.

"You could come to the house," I say. "I could call Aunt Julia. She wouldn't mind, I'm sure. I—"

"No," he snaps. Then softer, "No. I just—" He looks at me, his sudden anger slipping into urgency. "She'd want to talk to me. Ask me stuff. Want to talk about—"

"Your dad," I finish.

He nods. "And— I didn't tell you but I'm supposed to be in Venice. My mum paid for the ticket. But I didn't want to go. Not after … everything. And so I lied. I told her I was getting the train, so it would take longer, give me some time, you know? But instead I came here. I wanted to come here. I wanted to— I don't know… See Bea? And see you. Do you understand?"

My heart surges, a soaring thing, with wings of gold. For I do understand. I do.

I don't court it, this feeling. I don't even know if he shares it, or begins to. But I'm sure of one thing, one thing that brought us here, and now ties us, and that is Bea.

We sit on the deck – our hands splayed on the wood, close but not touching; our feet pale, ghost-like as they dangle in the water – and we talk about her. The easy stuff at first: her insistence that *Casablanca* was her favourite film, yet it was *Pretty in Pink* that she watched over and over again, until the video got stuck in the player; the time she added a bottle of blue-black ink to the bath to turn us into mermaids, and we wandered about like cyanotic waifs for a week until it finally washed off; the time she painted his face with her lipstick and rouge, crowned him with her Cleopatra wig, and they went down to a club in Deptford, teetering on costume department heels, giggling into vodka-tonics as, in the dingy lights and drunkenness, they almost, almost got away with the disguise.

Then the harder things: how she would disappear into her head for hours, sometimes days, living out a fiction she had created for herself – the consumptive Gothic heroine, the heroin-ravaged rock star. She would refuse to speak unless it was in character, unless you acknowledged this make-believe as a reality. She would talk as though to an invisible audience that she carried with her at all times, to witness her every word, her every move, because she had this skewed belief that there was no point doing anything if nobody was there to watch you do it.

"That's why I have to be in London," she wrote. "Because it's life itself, because it bursts with people to watch and be watched by. Eden kills me. It's like a morgue. I don't know how you stand it any more."

Penn shrugs when I tell him this. "Some people need to escape, that's all. Run away. No matter where they're from."

"Like you," I say. "Coming here."

"Yeah. I guess."

"Did you run away before? To college, I mean. Was that what it was?"

He pauses. "I think we all did," he says finally.

I imagine Bea and Penn and their friends, all of them fugitives, lost and found in their new world of bars and clubs and theatres and all the thrill of the fair. And for a second, just a second, I feel the ugly green of envy colour me.

But it wasn't all perfect in London, was it? There was the row. The one that drove her away. The one he wrote about in the letter.

I hated him for it at first. For upsetting her. But now; now I see. He was confused, hurt, his dad was dying. It was understandable – whatever it was. And forgiveable. He needs to know he is forgiven, by someone.

"It's OK," I tell him.

"What is?" he asks.

"Whatever happened between you and Bea. I'm not prying. Just … I'm sure she would have forgiven you."

"Like she forgave you?"

I feel my chest tighten. "Yes, I… It's complicated."

"What did you fight over?"

I pause.

"It's OK, you don't have to."

"No. It's not that." It's not. I do want to tell, I just want to find the right words. Words that don't render me the fool I am— was.

"A boy," I say at last. "Just a boy." Then add quickly, "He meant nothing to her. That was why I was angry, I think."

I'm scared I've said the wrong thing, shouldn't have brought up Tom at all.

But when he speaks, it's soft, sweet, not bitter. "I was like that," he says. "Until Bea. She changed everything."

"You did for her," I blurt. "She told me. She said you were…" I trail off, embarrassed now.

"I was what?" he asks.

I look down – searching for something: courage, honesty – then meet his eyes. "The One. She said you were The One."

He looks at me, lets the words sit there for one second, two, three. Then: "We should eat."

And so we do, carving up bread with a pocket knife as if we are castaways on an island, or smugglers hiding from the king's men.

Or from Tom.

He works in the mornings, so our hours at the creek are safe from spies, but every afternoon he comes to the house to see what I need: food, drink, company, maybe. I tell him the same list every time: milk, a loaf, more cheese. He never asks why I'm eating so much. Maybe he thinks

I'm feeding the mice, or the gulls that wheel above the water hoping for fish and ending up with chip wrappers.

"Are you OK?" he asks.

"Better," I reply. "Getting better."

And I am, I'm sure of it. Because of Penn.

I don't know what Penn does when I'm at Eden. I want to stay, to watch what happens, hidden in the woods – his invisible audience. But I have to play out my charade to Tom, keep Penn from Julia – keep any boy from Julia, for she'd think I was too young or too delicate. And so I do what I have to, day after day. As the sun grows stronger, and the days seem dizzy with light, as time slows, as the armies of ants abandon their long march at midday, and even the flies can manage no more than slow, drunken arcs, I go back to the dark of Eden.

Until one afternoon, my stomach heavy with bread and my head with the shandy I have found in the pantry, I fall asleep.

When I wake it's late. The sun is high in the sky – it is two now, three even. Time to go.

"Shit." I stagger to my feet, begin to gather my things, gather the evidence – bottles, a cracker packet, a can. A hand grasps mine, pulls me down again.

"Don't go."

"I have to," I say, snatching up the rest of the rubbish, stuffing it into my bag. "I have to see someone. This – this friend of Julia's." It's not a lie. He is. "If I'm late he'll come looking for me. And he'll find you."

"Just half an hour. We could swim," he says. "Please?"

And I know I cannot leave. I let my hands drop to my sides, let the bag slip from my shoulder to the floor.

"I knew you would," he says.

I've swum in the creek since I was four; learnt to swim here. I have jumped off the pontoon in black school swimsuits, and gold bikinis; have even once, as a dare, dived in topless. And yet now I can't take off my T-shirt because I'm embarrassed at what is underneath. Because I'm not her. Because underneath the black cotton triangles and beaded straps, I'm still a child; skinny, etiolated, my breasts barely more than the buds I had aged twelve. While she was a blossoming 32D, full-flowered at fifteen.

I was a freak, I thought, a weirdo. I would look at Alice Cordwainer's black C-cups spilling brazenly out of her top drawer, while I stuffed back the horror of my white 30A Cross Your Heart behind my knee socks and knickers. And then I would lie, late at night in the dorm, and trade impossible promises for breasts.

"Please God make them grow and I will eat all my cauliflower at supper."

"Please God make them grow and I will never ever swear again, not even if Bea tells me to."

"Please God make them grow and I will believe in you for ever."

But God had other fish to fry – Petra Deeds' missing periods, Holly Stanton's fat thighs, Bea's playing Mary in the school play – and he didn't hear my pleas, or chose to ignore them.

I take off my shorts but leave my T-shirt on, pull it down over my bikini bottoms.

"Take it off," he says. "You'll get soaked."

"It's fine," I say quickly. "I'm just— cold. I'm a bit cold."

He shrugs. It's thirty degrees, maybe more. But he doesn't question me. Just smiles, and then steps backwards, walking to the water's edge as if he will balance, Jesus-like, on the surface.

But he is flesh and bone, and he sinks, a mere human after all, then rises a few seconds later, laughing as his arms bring with them a tangle of weed, the slick green fronds clinging to his skin and hair.

"Poseidon," he yells. "I'm Poseidon."

Not Jesus, then. A god.

"Come on," shouts the god. "Come in."

And so I do. I close my eyes, and I jump.

We swim slowly, silently, circling each other at first until he stops and stands in the falling tide, and watches me, waits for me.

I feel his eyes on me as I plough through the water, my arms reaching from breaststroke to crawl. I'm trying to shake the adrenalin that runs through me, tainting my blood, heating it. My feet skim the bottom, sending a swirl of sand up to the surface, so that I don't see him reach out for me. He pulls me towards him. And then we are both standing, facing each other as if we're in a ballroom, not the middle of a river. I drop my head, so that he can't see what I'm thinking, but he brings it up again, raising my chin in his hand, moving it to touch my cheek, my hair.

And then he says it, faltering, but sure. "You … you look like her."

I feel something shift in me, a giving, and I cannot tell if it is relief, or sorrow.

"I don't."

"You do. That day— the first day. I thought it was her. I really thought…"

"Sorry to disappoint," I say.

"Oh, but you didn't," he insists. "You don't."

"I miss her," I say.

"I miss her, too. But—"

"But what?"

"We…" But he trails off. And then we are wrapped in silence, waiting for the next step, the inevitable step.

And I could take it. I could wrap my fingers in his hair, pull his face down towards mine. I could close my eyes, wait for his breath, warm on my wet skin, his lips on mine.

But in the distance the four o'clock ferry sounds its low lament across the bay, and the silence is shattered, the moment gone.

"I have to get back," I blurt.

And without waiting for an answer, without waiting to see if he follows me, I swim hard and fast back to the boat-house. I haul myself up on the deck, then, still dripping, my shorts and shoes in my hands, I run away.

Away from the possibility.

Away from the what ifs.

What if we kissed?

What if he loved me?

What if I loved him?

I run barefoot, stones digging into my soles, their sharp edges tearing into my skin. I run as if my life, my soul depended on it. Maybe it does. He is – he was – Bea's. That's a lifetime of Hail Marys or an eternity in hell, surely. I run without looking back, and without looking where I'm going.

And I run, of course I run, straight into Tom.

I panic, scrabbling for the shoes that I've dropped on the ground, as I scrabble for something to say.

"Hot, huh?" I manage, the words sounding like the panting of a dog.

Nothing.

"I— I went swimming."

"No shit."

I play a last desperate card. "We could go some time. Together. Maybe."

But it's not enough. He laughs, a short, mirthless sound. "Who is he?" he demands.

"Who's who?" I try, as I go through the moments in my head. Replaying them, trying to work out what he's seen. How much he's seen.

"Oh come on, Evie. Don't treat me like that. I saw you. You and him."

I feel my fear – of being found out, of Penn having to leave, of losing this— this whatever it is – turn to bitterness and anger. "It's none of your business. Not any more."

"What are you saying? That we're not friends any more? That it would have been my business, if what— if…"

"Say it," I say. "If you hadn't kissed her. Just admit it. Jesus."

"Yes, I kissed her. Because I was drunk and confused and I couldn't have what I really wanted. All right? Happy now?"

"No," I snap. "No, I'm not happy. It was the next day, Tom. Like, hours later."

"I know," he blurts. Then quieter, "I know," he repeats.

"We both made a mistake, OK? It was … it was never meant to be. For any of us."

"You mean that?"

Do I? Ten days ago, a week, it would have been a lie, a big fat lie. But now. I think of Penn, of what he is, and what he might be.

"Yes. We were friends. That's all."

"We can still be."

I look up at him from under a curtain of dripping hair. "If you were my friend, then you'd leave me be."

He shakes his head. "Fuck's sake, Evie."

The word digs into me, biting. Not because I haven't heard it before – Bea and I practised it, rolled it in our mouths, the delicious forbiddenness of it – but because I have never heard Tom say it. Not once. Not when his gutting knife slipped and he sliced into the top of his finger, his blood coagulating on the scales of a dead bass, mixing with its own. Not when I told him about the divorce. Not when he saw Bea with John Penrice the day after she'd kissed him.

I've gone too far, and I need to pull it back in, before it – this row – becomes a thing I cannot control at all.

"Have you told Julia?" I ask.

"No."

"Don't," I say. "Please. It's— he's a friend of Bea's. From uni. His name's Penn. Will Pennington. We're just— We talk. About her, OK?"

He pauses, and I wonder if he believes me. If he knows who Penn really was to Bea; if she told Hannah that Christmas when she came over. If she told him.

But if he knows, he doesn't let on. "How long is he staying?"

"I don't know."

"Evie—"

"I don't."

"Just be careful," he says finally.

"I will," I say. "I am."

But that night I can't sleep. In a bid to drive out the damp and dry out the paint, the decorators have switched on the central heating, so that Eden, once my stone-cold sanctuary, has become a suffocating hothouse. With heaving, complaining effort, rusting radiators churn a metallic fug into every room, filling halls and corridors with their groaning and clanking, like a ghost in chains.

I throw the windows wide in desperation, gulp down the night air as if it's a thirst, this feeling. I count sheep, count stars, count threads on the counterpane. But I can't keep him out, and the sheep scatter to make room for Penn. My head is full of him, pressing its own internal shutter on an album of snapshots: Penn in close-up, squinting into the sun, CLICK; Penn asleep on the deck, a tidemark of salt tracing a bracelet around his wrist, CLICK; Penn in the water, his hand touching my hair, his lips touching mine—

I stop myself. The camera has lied. That didn't happen. That can't happen.

A wave of disgust washes over me. Because he's not mine to kiss, he's Bea's— *was* Bea's. And it's not me he wants, it's her. I'm just a poor facsimile, a hastily drawn copy, like a child's rendition of the Mona Lisa. You can see who I'm supposed to be, but the lines are wrong, there are details missing, the nose is slightly too big, the smile lopsided. And yet, and yet…

"Tell me what to do, Bea," I say. "Help me." But though I say it aloud I know she won't answer. That this is down to me. Everything is down to me now.

I think back to Tom in the woods. His warning. "Be careful," he said. And I make a pact with myself. Tomorrow I won't go to the boathouse. Tomorrow I'll stay here at Eden. I'll stay with Bea. I'll sort out her treasures for her before it's too late. I'll put them in a box and seal it tight, so that I can take them with me when I go. Nothing happened between me and Penn. And nothing will happen. It's fine. I'm fine.

And yet even as I say the words, I see his face again, and I know it's useless. I'm not saved at all, I think. I'm drowning. And, worse, I chose to jump. I chose this fate.

Or maybe it chose me.

MAY 1988

BEA LIES *face down on the bed, in the almost-dark of drawn curtains and pale morning light. She is swimming in sound – in scorn, and spat-out words and a door slammed in anger. Its thin, bitter fluid envelops her, so that she shivers despite the mild May air.*

Penn's father has got worse. The cures have failed and now he's in hospital a hundred miles away in Hampshire, a frail shell of the man who hailed colleagues in the soft-carpeted corridors, who downed glass after glass of red wine and talked loudly of Thatcher on the terrace.

"Please come," Penn begs her. "I need you."

"You don't," she replies. "You'll be fine. Besides, I can't, I have to rehearse." But this is a lie and they both know it, for

the play is still weeks away. But she can't tell him the truth because it's pathetic and reveals her to be lacking, cruel even.

She went with him to the hospital before. Imagining the urgency of a hospital drama, she painted herself Florence Nightingale in the picture; an angel sent to revive him and reconcile him with his prodigal son. But the reality bore no resemblance to her version. There were no dashing doctors, no heartfelt "sorry"s; just endless waiting in corridors hung with the smell of disinfectant and death.

"I suppose you'll be seeing James?" he says.

"I don't know. Maybe. What does it matter?"

But it does matter. Today she needs to see him, to get away from this stifling, choking thing she is trapped in. Not Penn, she tells herself. It's not Penn she's escaping. But even so, when James arrives an hour later, she follows him out of the house, feeling sweet release as the door slams behind her for the second time that day, knowing there will be no more raised voices, no suffocating silences, no pretence that they can't see death lurking at the door. For Bea needs life. Penn will understand that. Penn will forgive her for that. Eventually.

"Where are we going?" she asks.

"On a magical mystery tour," he promises with a bow and a flourish.

Bea laughs. "The Taj Mahal? The Hanging Gardens of Babylon?"

"No."

"Bibendum then, to eat a dozen oysters? Or ice cream – knickerbocker glories at Joe's?"

"Nope."

She sighs with mock disappointment, shakes her head. "No class, that's your problem."

"Class and money aren't the same thing," he says suddenly.

She reddens with sudden, unfamiliar embarrassment. "I didn't mean... It was a joke. You're all class." And she links her arm through his.

"This?" she asks, not even bothering to hide the distaste. "Seriously? This is it?"

They're on the edge of a Peckham estate. Four blocks of grey, no-hope flats tower over them, grim sentinels keeping watch over a landscape of broken glass and no ball games.

"Close your eyes," he tells her. Then he moves behind her and places his palms over her face.

"No." She pulls away and turns to face him. "You're scaring me now."

"Don't be scared. You have to trust me."

"I—"

He takes her hands in his and grips them tight. "Do you trust me?" he asks, and his face is etched with such urgency, such need, that there can only be one answer.

"Yes," she whispers. "Yes, I trust you."

And so she shuts her eyes, and lets him take her by the hand and lead her blindly forward. She trips through the empty cans and overflowing bins, through the high-rises and low lives, until she hears the sounds change: the flat, concrete hollowness becomes a softer, kinder thing and his voice, calm now, tells her, "This is it. We're here."

She opens her eyes and starts. Her mouth falls open and her breath pulls in sharply as if she is about to speak, but there are no words. Instead she nods, bewildered. Because it's a kind of magic trick he has pulled, a sleight of hand, for she's no longer on a sink estate surrounded by graffitied walls and boarded windows, cars held together with gaffer tape and prayer, like the lives of those who own them, borrow them, steal them. Instead there are trees – oaks, a silver birch, a dark, berry-hung yew; a lawn, overgrown, its soft fabric sequined with buttercups and daisies; and, down a nettle-choked path, a summerhouse, its pale, sandstone cupola sheltering two painted wooden benches. She has gone from bitter browns and dead greys to this green, this life.

"I—" she falters.

"My secret garden," he says.

"How did you find it?" she manages at last.

"I got lost," he says. "And I found this."

James doesn't tell her why he was lost. Walking gets rid of the rage he feels when he sees her with Penn. And he walks most days, sometimes all day, and has covered the length and breadth of the city, from the clipped, cloistered afternoon suburbia of Penge to the flashing lights and fucking of late-night Soho. He's walked from the sound of Bow bells to the shadow of Big Ben, has walked past stucco townhouses and through

*prefab estates. He's seen this entire city's ugliness, but some-
times, he comes across a place of pure, staggering beauty, a
place paved with gold. Like this.*

"Eden," she says. "It's Eden."

*He shakes his head. "Better than," he says. "Because this
is real."*

*"No," she says quickly. "No, you don't understand. Eden,
it's where I live, in the holidays, anyway. The house in
Cornwall?"*

*He nods, remembering. She showed him a picture once, of
her on a boat. Bea was standing, precarious in a pink dress, a
big, out-of-place thing with a bodice and beads, while another
figure, her T-shirted back to the camera, rowed her to shore.*

*Tears spill down Bea's cheeks, black rivulets of mascara
running across pale skin.*

*"What is it? Do you miss it?" His concern is urgent. Be-
cause these tears are real, not the crocodile ones she keeps
for the stage, or made of the liquid glycerine she keeps in her
pocket for the rare times she is unmoved. This is unmanu-
factured sorrow, grief even, that doesn't fit with the story she
has told of boredom, of counting down endless, pointless days
until she could be here, in London. "I thought you didn't
want to go back? You stayed here all Easter. You could have
gone, if you'd wanted. Couldn't you?"*

She shakes her head. "We had a row."

*"Your mam?" he blurts, his concern letting the word slip
out, a single syllable betraying the past he has worked so hard
to escape.*

But wrapped in her own worry, she doesn't notice. "No," she says. "Evie. My—"

"… cousin," he finishes.

"You know about her?" she says.

Of course he does. He's overheard this piece of information and kept it safe; a jewel to admire, Fagin-like, when he is alone.

She wipes her face on her arm, transferring a smudge of black to the thin, green cotton of her cardigan. "It was a stupid thing, last summer. My fault," she adds quickly. "Then I should have stayed longer at Christmas. But there was Penn. And then at Easter we had the festival the first week, and after that, I don't know, it just got harder. I did write to her. Twice. Or three times maybe. But she never wrote back."

"She doesn't own you," he tells her, angry that someone could try to monopolize her, take her away from him.

"No. I know. It's just … it goes back further. We were like sisters, and then— and then we weren't. And I let it happen. I let it drift. She said she'd never forgive me."

He doesn't believe her. Who could not forgive this goddess? He, he would forgive her anything; does forgive her anything. He feels a surge of an idea inside him – a way to help both of them. To get her away from Penn, this boy who is ruining her, breaking her.

"So go back. I'll come with you. We'll go now!"

But Bea shakes her head. "She won't be there. She's at school."

"Oh."

"I could write?" she says.

He thinks of the letter his sister Brigid has sent. Thinks of how she must have called the college, begged for his address. But he doesn't want to hear about her sorry life: the new husband and the nights down the John Bull and the days on the line at the sweet factory. Doesn't want to tell her about his brilliant one. Not until it is just that – until it is the shining thing he always said it would be.

But Bea's life is already gleaming.

"Can I be in your Eden?" he asks.

"Yes. You can have a lead part. You can be Prospero."

"And this is our island," he declares. "Our Eden. Our paradise."

Bea smiles, and lets him lead her into the garden. He shows her the orchids like bees, the mosaics patterning the paths, the wild parakeets. She is happy. She will write to Evie again. She'll tell her she misses her. That she can't wait to see her, can't wait to be at Eden. That it will be like it was before, for all of them – her and Evie and Tom. That she will make it right between them, she will.

But later, as they sit in the summerhouse and the light fades and air cools, Bea realizes that this perfect day will soon be gone, and she knows that she won't write. Not again. Her life is here now. Has to be here.

Her and Penn. Not Evie. Penn.

AUGUST 1988

I'M WOKEN by the phone. Its insistent trill cuts shrilly through the fog of sleep, a cruel alarm clock. I fumble for my watch on the dressing table, open one eye. It's twenty past eight. "Who would call at this time?" I think. "Who would call at all?"

And then I'm wide awake, sat bolt upright. Aunt Julia. Aunt Julia would call. Because Tom's told her about Penn. And she wants to know what's going on. What do I think I'm playing at? Why is he staying there? Where is he sleeping? Where am I sleeping? I hear her questions bombard me in my head.

Or maybe it's not her but Penn's mother asking why he didn't take the train. Why he never made it to Venice.

The phone stops, and I feel minute, momentary relief, but then it starts again, each ring jabbing at me: get up, Evie, get up and explain yourself. I have to answer it. If I don't she'll ring again, and again until I do. I throw back the sheet and run across the landing in my vest top and knickers, my feet hitting every creaking board under the carpet then slapping against slate, the scratches from yesterday stinging with every step, reminding me, punishing me for that, for those feelings.

I'll tell her just enough and no more, I think. I'll say he was a friend of Bea's. Just a friend. It's the truth, I lie.

I pick up the green receiver, and brace myself. "Hello?"

"Evie?"

The voice is cut-glass, the kind that orders gin and tonic or a Martini shaken, not stirred. It's her.

And it's me. "Yes," I say. "Yes, it's Evie."

"Well who else would it be, I suppose." Her voice sounds resigned. Not angry. Just, well, resigned.

I try to laugh. But it sounds odd, more like a cough. As if I have forgotten how.

"Are you ill?"

"No," I reply quickly. "I'm fine. Everything's fine."

"Well, good. That's good."

We speak for five minutes. Five minutes of "are you eating enough?" and "how is the weather?" and "have they started the bedrooms yet?" Five minutes of saying nothing. Because there is nothing to explain. Tom didn't call. He didn't tell her.

I'm safe.

So why do I feel anything but?

I try to stay in. I try to shutter myself inside the foot-thick granite walls of Eden, and ignore the call of the creek, the call of him.

I take clothes from the dryer, mechanically fold them into piles: socks, knickers, T-shirts. I make myself toast, cut it into soldiers, chew methodically on one before tipping the rest in the bin. I watch the decorators with their tins of hide-all magnolia, offer to help. But it's suffocating, all of it: the repetitive slap-slop of paint on walls, the inane sing-song of the radio, the creeping change with every completed wall or window frame. My chest is tight; the absurdity, the pointlessness of my efforts a vice around my ribcage. I can't breathe. The now-dry heat of the house has given way to a new humidity, the air heavy with the pressure of rain that will not fall, as if it is conspiring to taunt me, goad me into action.

As if it knows there's only one place I want to go.

I can see him sat on the deck facing the water, his back to me. He's writing something, a diary maybe, or a postcard. At the sound of my steps he stops, puts it away in his bag and turns to me.

And he smiles.

And my heart sings.

"I thought you weren't coming."

"I wasn't," I say. "But then I did." It's garble. But I can't say the words, can barely find them.

"You want to swim?"

I shake my head.

"Go somewhere then? Calenick?"

"Not Calenick," I say quickly. I couldn't stand people's quick, sly glances, nor their pity.

"Where then?"

"The point," I say.

"The point?"

"You'll see."

You can't walk to the point. There are no roads. Even from the right side of the river it's a two-mile hike through a tangle of thickets and barbed wire. From here, there's only one way to reach it: by boat.

My back to the sun, I pull hard on *Jorion*'s oars. The wood complains, creaking in the rowlocks: "Where have you been?" "Why have you forgotten us?"

But I'm here now— we're here. He leans back against the stern of the boat, watching me, as I watch him. He's changed. His skin is darker now, his hair blonder. He looks like a wild boy, a local. Or like Pan. The Pan of our imaginings.

The hull scrapes something, unseating him.

"Shit," I exclaim. "Sorry."

I turn to see the black of sea-slick rock. There are quick bursts of white, like smoke, as water shatters against its ragged edges, then settles. We're here.

I throw the painter out, and, jumping, follow it, tie it to the iron ring at the foot of the cliff, a relic from the tin trade maybe, or smugglers. Though Bea said it was left for us, put there especially.

"So this is it," he says.

"Are you disappointed?"

"No. Never."

"It's a climb though."

"I like heights."

You'd have to. The point is forty feet up and a slow, tripping, slipping scramble over rocks and sea thrift. Then at the top there's nothing but a wide plateau, weather-beaten into smoothness by Atlantic wind and rain. But it's not the point we're here for, it's what you can see from it.

Everything. I can see everything.

I can see the arc of Pont Cove, its pale, gritty sand studded with the reds and greens of children's swimsuits, hunched determinedly over castles and ignoring the gathering clouds.

I can see our creek, a little finger extended from the hand of the river estuary, the middle finger pointing inland, past the docks to the big towns, and then London beyond.

And I can see the house, held like a jewel in the gloved palm of the trees; the slant of its roof, the breadth of its walls, the whole breathtaking beauty of its existence.

"Is that…?" he trails off.

"Eden," I say. "That's Eden."

"It's something."

I shake my head. "No. It's everything. It's perfect. Why would she want to leave? Look around you. Look!" I demand. "Why would she need to run away from this?"

"I don't know," he says finally.

But I do. Because even in its vastness and perfection, it wasn't enough. I wasn't enough.

I hear a rumble in the distance, a clatter of clouds against each other and I feel the crackle of electricity in the air.

"Rain's coming," I say. "We should go."

I stand, turn towards the stepped rocks that stand for a path.

"Isn't there another way down?"

I shake my head. "Other side's too steep," I say.

"I didn't mean that. It's safe, isn't it? I mean the water's deep here?"

"Yes, but—"

"Have you done it before?"

"No." But others have. Coffin jumping they call it. The boys from the village come on Saturdays, pumped full of a heady mix of bravado and cheap cider. They are loud and lairy and look-at-me as they leap into the unknown. And Bea has done it too, once, her hand tight in the grip of a boy called Gregor – that year's love.

"So come on then. First time for everything."

I look down. Maybe it's not so far, I tell myself. Maybe

it's deep enough – the tide is high, isn't it? And he's here. He's with me.

"Aren't you scared?" I ask.

"I used to be," he admits. "When I was a kid." He pauses. "Actually, even this year. We went to this lido, me and Bea and— and some others. She jumped from the high board. God, you should have seen her, Evie. She looked incredible. But me, I— I let her down, I guess. But not today. We're going to fly," he adds. "Like Icarus."

I look at him. "But there's no sun," I say.

And then he takes my hand. "You're my sun," he says.

Juliet, I think. I am the East and Juliet is my sun.

And I trust him.

I believe him.

I believe in him.

And I jump.

The fall takes no time and for ever. It's a rush that turns my insides and sends my blood retreating into my farthest flesh and then back to flood my heart again. I'm in a vortex in which the world has stopped turning then spins in fast-forward. I hit water. The impact is swift and loud. It wrenches our hands apart and sends a geyser of water skywards, through which we plummet into a sudden, tumbling descent. I throw my arms out, try to right myself, but I can't see which way is up and which is down. I can't hear anything but the muffled roar of my own blood in my ears and I can't breathe, as the water has pushed every ounce of air out of my lungs.

I'm going to die, I think. I'm going to die and I don't care, because I've flown. For just a few seconds, I've felt what it is to be weightless, without burden.

I see a light in front of me. This is it, I think. This is the end. And I swim towards it.

But God has other plans.

Because when I reach out to the light I don't feel the heat of a heaven but coldness. Air.

I burst through the surface of the water, gasping for breath with which to scream. Because I need to scream. Not with terror, but something else. I need to tell the world I'm here, I exist, I'm alive.

"See me, world? See me now?" I yell. "Do you?"

"Evie!"

I turn and he's there. Alive too.

"See," he says, his eyes wide with delight, with relief, maybe. "We did it. You did it. You can do anything you want. Be anyone you want."

I smile. Because I did do it. We did it. Together. I showed him. I helped him. And he helped me.

And I smile because that's what Bea said. That I could do anything, be anyone. And I never believed her until now. Now I know Penn is right. And I know exactly who I want to be.

We're still only halfway across the creek when the rain starts to fall: fat heavy drops at first, slow and unsure; then harder, definite. By the time we reach the boathouse the base of *Jorion* is inches-deep in sea and stormwater. We reach the bank as the first peal of thunder echoes up the river, urging us to move faster as we haul *Jorion* to the bank then slip over wet decking in our haste to take shelter.

We burst through the door of the boathouse, stumbling, breathless, and slam the door behind us in relief. Then there is a pause, comic timing, and we look at each other and laugh. Because it's still raining.

I look up and realize why: the plastic bags we stuffed into the holes in the rusted roof have blown away and great spouts of rain are pouring down onto the camp bed. The sleeping bag has been stained a deep wine colour and Penn's clothes are a sodden mass.

"Shit," he exclaims, as his eyes follow mine. He pulls the bed to one side and then begins wringing out a pair of jeans.

"No," I say. "Don't."

"What?"

"There's no point."

"But I've got nothing to wear," he protests. "Nowhere to sleep."

I shake my head. "It's fine. Come with me."

"Where are we going?"

I take a breath. "Eden."

"But—"

But I don't let him finish. Not this time. For suddenly I'm someone else. I am Bea. I can feel her inside me, feel a gloss, a glimmer to the dullness, hear her voice now, clear and commanding.

"We're going to Eden."

And he must see her in me. For he is meek now, allows me to lead. "Are you sure?" he asks.

"I'm sure," I reply.

I have never been surer.

JUNE 1988

IT'S LATE *when they get back to Telegraph Hill – gone ten. Their throats are sore from talking and from acting scenes in the park for an audience of pigeons, and their fingers sting with salt and vinegar from the bag of chips they have shared.*

"Come in," she says. "He's away until tomorrow. Not that that makes a difference," she adds quickly.

James feels that same sharp needling in his side at her mention of Penn. But he doesn't want the day to end, so he swallows his irritation and lets her lead him inside.

But someone else has got there first again.

As they tumble, stumble through the door, a voice halts their footsteps, cuts their laughter short.

"Where've you been?"

Penn is on her bed, his hands so tight around the neck of a half-gone bottle of vodka that his knuckles are white, while his eyes are wide, the pupils black in the failing light.

"You're back?" she says, putting her arms around him.

"Clearly." Penn shrugs her off but James can see it is bravado and is meant to pull her in further, away from him.

"But I thought—"

"Yeah. Well you thought wrong."

"I was just out with James. Just James," she repeats.

Just James. He wishes they were outside again, where the streets are golden and he isn't "just" anybody. He wants to be her knight in shining armour; for her to ask him to take her away from all this. But she's not Rapunzel in her locked tower waiting for a prince to rescue her. She can leave if she pleases.

But she doesn't please.

"Oh, baby," she laments, stroking Penn's hair. "How's your dad?"

"Bad." Penn drops the bottle, touches his hand to her face.

James hears the scrape and sputter of a match strike inside his head. The hard ball of pain inside him catches on the flame.

"Will you be OK?" he asks. "Should I stay?" He looks at Bea then at the vodka bottle. It is a "leave now, come with me" look.

But she won't.

"Go on," she says softly. "Go. I'll be fine. I'll see you in the morning."

* * *

As he treads back down the darkened hall, he feels the flames take hold, burning through him. Penn is the cat that got the cream. While he, James, the faithful dog, gets nothing. Just the sour, thin whey that is left behind. He won't sleep tonight. He'll walk the night-abandoned streets of the city, until he's cold and tired and spent.

But even as he takes his first step he knows that, in the cold light of the morning, she'll still be there, a bright-glowing ember, refusing to turn to ash. And he knows that he'll never give up. Never walk away.

Never let her go.

AUGUST 1988

WE'RE AT the kitchen table, me in a black dress and him in a borrowed T-shirt. Towels are draped over the chairs and our wet clothes are slung over radiators, sending up faint clouds of steam and the smell of washing powder and river water.

"Have you always lived here?"

I nod.

"But it was your grandparents' house, not your mum's?"

Normally I'd squirm at this, feel the question dig in like a poking finger, like a scalpel trying to cut a reluctant truth out of me. But in his hands, his voice, it's transformed into a key, and I let it unlock me. "Both," I say. "My mum never left home. Well, for college – art college – but then she came back. She died when I was three. Cancer. And I never knew my dad. I'm not even sure that she did. My grandparents raised me. And Bea, kind of. I went to school in the village and she came here in the holidays. But then they died, and I got sent to school too."

"Boarding school?"

"Yeah. But not like Malory Towers at all." I smile, thinking of the scorn and the whispers and the impossible hierarchy that I couldn't fathom, much less climb. "Enid Blyton lied," I add.

"But Bea was there. Didn't she look after you?"

"Some," I say. Because she tried. But we were in different dorms and different years. And while age differences disappear like smoke on summer beaches, in school corridors they are a uniform, are everything, as important and defining as your shoes, the contents of your pencil case, and whether your daddy wears a navy pinstripe suit or white overalls. So I watched as she negotiated sports days and secret clubs and school shows with the ease of a chameleon, while I, ungainly, awkward, stood at the edges. "She just kind of fitted in. Or stood out, maybe."

"And you?"

I laugh. "I just disappeared." Made myself disappear. A shadow of Bea.

"But you must have gone to boarding school," I say. "You must know what it's like?"

I wait for him to talk then. Because he's been taken away from his family, and had his family taken from him.

And not in this distant, daydream manner that my own early losses have become. But he doesn't take the bait. Not yet. He's still watching the lure dance in front of him.

"They were rich, then?"

"My grandparents? I guess. Though you wouldn't know it to look at them." Dressed in dog-dirty corduroy for most of the time. But there were parties. I remember walking through a sea of stocking-clad legs, over patent-leather heels and dark polished brogues, navigating my way to a table with its cut-glass bowls of peanuts and Twiglets. Though those stopped long ago. After my grandmother died. Julia tried to throw her own; invited crowds of Henrys and Ginnys over from Rock or down from London. But she put out bitter tasting olives instead of crisps, wine instead of sweet sherry. And, banished upstairs, Bea and I would watch from the landing, our legs hanging through the banisters, imagining affairs for the women, dastardly deeds for the men.

"They weren't, you know, Lord and Lady or anything though," I continue. "The house was built for an earl, I think, but he gambled, and my great, great grandfather, he won the house in a game of Black Jack." Or so the story went. But like so many stories my grandfather told, the lines between fact and fiction blurred, and truth got tangled in something more interesting.

He laughs. "That's incredible."

I nod.

"And now it's your aunt's?"

I shake my head quickly. "Mine actually. Well, mine and Bea's. He left it to us. That's why we still came back in the holidays, all holiday. It was in the will – that it had to be our home and we had to spend the holidays here."

"Clever."

"Not really. Aunt Julia hated coming here and Uncle John never had the time. And Grandpa didn't leave any money to look after it, and so now, well, it has to be sold. They win."

"That's not fair."

I shrug. "Life's not fair," I say, echoing Aunt Julia's excuse, her get-out clause, trying to appear devil-may-care.

But I do care, and he knows it.

"We were going to live here, me and Bea," I tell him. "When we grew up, I mean. We were going to have a wing each. She was going to put on plays, turn it into a theatre or a film set."

"What were you going to do?"

"Take the tickets." It sounds like nothing. Like the job you give to the smallest child, or the fool, to keep them out of the way. But it wasn't like that; Bea wasn't like that. I chose it. I was happy to stay in the wings as long as I could watch her. And then, when the audiences were gone, it would be ours again, our own stage. It never occurred to me that by then we'd have grown out of those games, out of make-believe.

He folds then unfolds his arms, then leans forward. "What about … men – boyfriends?" His face reddens as he says it. It's the first time I've seen him falter or show a flicker of embarrassment. I wonder why now. Is it because of Bea? Or me?

"They'd have been brothers," I say. "And best friends. They'd have gone along with it. Living here, the four of us." Bea said this once, had this idea we would meet and marry twins, that we would all live together, our children interchangeable, sleeping in one giant nursery.

But the truth was that, until she met Penn, the men in Bea's life played only bit parts: trees or soldiers. Like swifts or swallows, they came and went with the seasons. She was the star of this imagined life, and I her faithful side-kick. I'd thought, once, in my own idle daydreaming, that we wouldn't need to marry brothers. I could marry Tom. He would inherit the Millhouse and work for us. Then one day I'd kiss him – this frog prince – and then we two would tend to Bea, together, for ever.

I feel my own face redden at my childish conceit, my foolishness, and change the subject. "I'll show you where you're sleeping," I say. "You can have the blue room."

"The blue room." He repeats. "It's like a film, or a novel. 'She slept in the yellow room, he in the blue.'"

There's an edge in his voice. Sarcasm. Jealousy almost.

"Sorry," I mumble, as I lead the way to the staircase. "I know it sounds – I don't know… lame."

"No, no." He turns to me. "I didn't mean it like that. It's just so different. That's all. Different."

"Not like this at yours then?"

He laughs. "No."

"I thought you had a big house – Hampshire isn't it?"

"I— yes, yes we do. In the constituency. But I was thinking of London."

"Of course," I say. Then mumble a "sorry". Because I shouldn't have taken him back to his house – it's a place I don't want to go either.

"You don't have to be sorry." He looks down. "I'm the sorry one."

I want to tell him then – that it wasn't his fault, it couldn't have been; he wasn't even there. It was an accident. No one could have known what was going to happen. I want to squeeze his hand so he knows it's all right. Or is going to be. That one day it will be no more than a memory, as distant and air-light as the others. It has to be.

But maybe it's me who needs convincing.

We've climbed the staircase now, risen from the paint pots and wallpaper tables of the ground floor to the wide, galleried landing of the first, where the walls remain untouched, keeping their faces for just a few more days. For that's all we have: a few more days until he, and then I, will have to move on.

I push the thought down and grasp the brass handle in front of me. "This is it," I say, and I turn the handle slowly, then push the door and let it swing open. I let him step into the room first and see it in its strange, sad glory.

"It was my grandparents' room," I say, explaining the

double bed, the brush set on the dressing table, the photographs on the window sill.

"It's great," he says. "Thanks."

But I know he's disappointed. Despite its splendour, its views across the lawns, its carpet so wide you can waltz across it, this isn't the room he wanted to see.

"I can take you up there." I say. "If you want?"

He nods, not even answering. He doesn't need to: I understand. Just as he understands me, knows me; like I know him.

And so, leaving his books and bag on the floor, we close the door and climb the narrow, twisting staircase to the attic.

For a while he says nothing, just silently touches these pretty, precious things with childlike wonder. Then it begins. Her baubles and bric-a-brac pull the sorrow from him on long ribbons of memory.

"I loved her," he says. "So much, but—" He pauses, to find the right words, to find the strength. He grasps a bottle of nail varnish. The rose red is set in stark contrast to the white of his knuckles. "We had a fight. A petty, pointless fight. I made a mistake, told a lie, and she … she couldn't forgive me."

I go to touch his hand. I want to unclench it because I am afraid he will shatter the glass and the polish will drip blood-like down his fingers. But he pulls away.

"But I loved her. You have to believe me. You do believe me, don't you?" He's desperate now, his eyes wide, whites showing. He drops the bottle and it hits the rug noiselessly. Then he clutches me instead, my arms in his hands, his grip tight, terrified. "Evie. Do you believe me?"

"Yes," I say. "Yes I believe you. I told you before, I told you: it's OK."

A sob breaks free from him then, and he drops onto the bed, his head hidden in his hands.

I sit beside him, unsure whether to touch him or if he'll lash out. But I have to do something so at last I pull him to me. And his face still hidden, he lets me hold him, gentle at first, but then more tightly, as if I can squeeze the hurt out; like a promise, that I will never let go.

And so we sit, for how long I'm not sure. Until the tears subside, until he's pulled away to wipe the salt from his face, the snot from his chin. And I know I can't lie any more. I don't want him to think he is alone in this.

"She hated me," I say suddenly. Blurting it out before I can change my mind.

He turns quickly, shakes his head, his brow creased in confusion. "No. She loved you."

"She did. Once. But then, after that row – about the boy – I couldn't forgive her. She apologized but I refused to listen. And so she dropped me."

For it wasn't just those three spat-out words over Tom on Christmas Eve, but another argument, two days later, as she was leaving. "Wake up," she'd said to me. "Wake up, or grow up. Either will do."

"You're the one who needs to grow up," I'd sneered back

at her, my childish whining destroying my own argument.

She'd rolled her eyes at that, taken her bag and stormed downstairs. I stayed in my room, watched the car pull away, saw her staring ahead, refusing to look up in case she saw my sorry face. It was the last time I saw her.

"But she wrote," he says.

I shake my head. Not after Christmas. I'd waited for a letter, checked my pigeonhole every day for an apology or even a pretence that nothing was wrong, a postcard of Big Ben with "wish you were here" on the back.

"Look at me," he says.

I raise my eyes to his.

"She was going to write," he says. "She told me. To say sorry. She wanted to come and see you in May, but you weren't here – you were at school. Then in July she said she was coming back to Eden. To wait for you. She was going to take a train, that night…" His voice cracks as he realizes what he has said, what this means to him, what it will do to me; that sickly sweet, almost-but-not-quite of it.

But I already know. Because he told me of her plans to come back in a letter I shouldn't have opened because it was never meant for me. A letter that's hidden now, pushed to the back of a drawer where I can't see it, where it can't harm me.

But as I go to betray it with a glance, something distracts me: a flicker in the corner of the room, a brush of air across my face.

"She's still here," I say.

"What?"

I blush again as I hear myself. I am idiotic, a cliché. "I just mean, I feel her sometimes, that's all. I know it sounds stupid." I try to get out of it, making excuses like a child caught red-handed.

"No," he says, his voice clear, sure. "It's not stupid." Then, for a moment, he is lost in himself. "So she came back, after all."

"Yes," I say.

He looks around, his eyes darting, as if he is searching the high ceiling, the canopy, the cornicing.

"Is she with us now?" he says. "Can you hear her?"

I listen, and there it is again, echoing from the walls, bouncing off the wood of the bookcase. She is speaking to me. For the first time she is speaking to me, saying the same words over and over, the same words that Tom used.

Be careful, Evie, she says. *Be careful.*

"No," I lie. "I can't hear anything."

JUNE 1988

THE WARDROBE *is dark, safe. It is the perfect place to hide.*

Another production has ended and another party has begun in the house on Telegraph Hill. James said he wasn't going this time and had waited for her to beg, plead, as he knew she would. Because she needs him now that she's losing Penn to the mess of his life; his dying father, his mother in denial.

So James makes the walk along Queens Road, a bottle of cheap red in a plastic bag and a white seed of hope in his heart. And he pretends he's one of them. He talks to them, drinks with them. Though all the time he knows he is a king amongst mortals, with their drugs and their too-loud laughs and their childish games. Someone even suggests hide and seek and Bea claps her hands and says she will be "it". So James agrees to play for her sake. He knows at once where he will hide.

For she doesn't share Penn's room any more, she has her own: the attic. A girl has moved out, off to a part in a Northern soap, and she has taken her place. She has hung her butterfly dresses across the eaves and set the mirror up under a high window, so that in one swift glance she can see her own reflection and that of the city – its promise mirrored in the burgeoning skyline of the Docklands, the first gleaming storeys of Canary Wharf.

"It makes sense for me to have my own room," she says. "That's all. Don't read anything into it."

And then she counts off the reasons she has chosen solitude: Penn has finals, he needs the quiet; next year he'll probably be away, in rep, and Hunter wants his room; she can see the river. But he knows these are just caulk, paper to cover a crack; only a chink now, tiny, but a vulnerability just the same, into which he can insinuate himself, can push his way deeper into her world, and push Penn out.

And so he is here, Narnia-like in her wardrobe, crouched among the coats and cardigans, all hung with the smell of her, the smell of patchouli and possibility. And just like always he waits for her to come to him at last.

AUGUST 1988

IN THE weeks without Bea, the house always seemed impenetrable; a fortress of thick, grey silence. In the days before she came home it wore an expectant air. Her bed would be turned down, the larder stocked with her favourite pink wafers, her wellington boots retrieved from the back of the garage and lined up in the hallway, waiting for her feet to slip inside. Like me they were waiting for adventure. Then, when she was here, Eden was transformed: every barren corridor became a secret passage; every plain wooden door a portal to a new world of wonder.

Now, with Penn, I feel it again. Eden is alive with possibility.

We breakfast on fig rolls and orangeade, sitting

cross-legged on a blanket box on the landing; we lie top to toe on the iron day bed, reading plays and poetry; we play parlour games and hide and seek like rainy-day children.

"It'll be fun," I insist, when he says it's childish. "You'll see."

And he does. And the decorators curse as we sneak under dustsheets and behind paint-tacky shutters. They beg us to go outside to play. So the next time, when it's my turn to hide, I slip past the open door and dance across the lawn to the stable block. Then I crouch down behind the sleek, curved wheel arch of a Jaguar, and wait.

At first all I hear is the thump-thump of my racing heart, but then it comes: the crunch of a shoe on gravel, cautious at first; two slow steps, then a pause while he surveys the kingdom, seeks his quarry. Then a run when he sees the doors are ajar, throwing a shaft of sunlight across the concrete floor.

"I know you're in there," he calls, his voice rising and falling like a moustache-twirling villain, like the Hooded Claw. "I'm coming to get you."

I feel my breath quicken as his footsteps get closer. I want to win, but I also want to be found.

He's behind me now. I see an elongated shadow stretch out before me; catch the piney smell of his deodorant, the faint peppermint of my toothpaste. I gasp as a pair of hands closes over my eyes, as lips brush my ear.

"Got you," he whispers.

Got me, I think. But I don't move. I don't try to flee.

Because I want this. And more.

We stay there, for one heartbeat, then two, then ten. Until suddenly his hands drop, and he stands.

"What is this place anyway?"

I scrabble to my feet and brush the dust from my hands onto my shorts while I shoo away the disappointment. "Oh, um, the stables. Well, it was," I elaborate, gushing now to cover. "But no one rode really after my mum. Well, I did a bit, but then there was school. So Uncle John put his cars in here."

There are four of them. Four vintage classics, all polished in a row. Barely driven; the tread of their wheels still deep, the leather unmarked. Uncle John's pride and joy. Locked up, shut away from the dangers of the world. Like he would've shut away Bea if he could, kept her like Rapunzel in her tower, until some handsome prince with a minor title and an account at Coutts rescued her and took her to his palace in Kensington.

But Bea was too wise for that. And she didn't need rescuing, she said. She could rescue herself. Though she still let them try, let them shower her with gifts and plaudits and pleas, gave them just enough to think they had won her hand and heart, then slammed the door and ran back to the attic, laughing all the way.

"Where are the keys?" he asks, his voice edged with excitement, with purpose now.

"What?"

"The keys for the cars?"

"In the cabinet. But it's locked," I say. Of course it's locked, with a combination set by Uncle John.

And solved by me and Bea one long Sunday when we were playing at codebreakers; she the wartime heroine, me an orphan child she had found and adopted. Not that we ever used it. It was the knowing that mattered, the beating the grown-ups at their own game.

"You know the number don't you," he says.

"I—"

"Come on. It will be fun."

"But I can't drive."

"I can."

"I shouldn't."

"You shouldn't," he echoes.

"I shouldn't," I repeat.

But I will.

And there they are: four numbers – the date of Bea's birthday – revealing four single keys to match four singular cars.

"Eeeny, meeny, miney, mo…" He runs his fingers along the hooks. "Catch a tiger by the toe."

"If he hollers let him go."

He smiles. "Eeeny, meeny, miney. Mo!"

He plucks the key from the wall, dangles it around his little finger. "So which one is it?" he asks, his accent changed. He is dapper now, Waughesque.

"That one," I say in perfectly clipped notes, a flapper to his Bright Young Thing. "The Alfa, darling."

We roll slowly down the long drive. "Don't race," I warn, echoing Uncle John to Julia. "The gravel will fly up and scratch the paint."

He laughs. "Scaredy cat."

I am scared. And excited. And horrified. And happy. Because I'm sat next to him in a 1969 cherry red Alfa Giulia, top down, radio on, heading through the iron gates of Eden towards the world, towards no-man's-land.

We come to a halt at the road.

"Which way?" he asks.

"Where do you want to go?"

"Where is there to go?"

"Right is England."

"What about left?"

I start, remembering the last time I came this way. "It's— town. Well, village really. Calenick."

I never liked it that much. Bea would beg me to go with her, to take our games of Cinderella or Macbeth to a bigger stage, where we could pass as kitchen girls or princesses or blood-handed queens amongst a wider audience.

"There's a whole world out there," she would say, her eyes lit with a strange kind of hunger. "All those people."

"In Calenick?" I would reply.

"It's a start," she would snap. And then sulk until she got her way. For she always got her way. And so she would make Calenick our Emerald City, or our Tara, and she wouldn't miss a beat: not a stumbled line or a skipped gesture as she walked up Fore Street, Elizabeth Taylor in a pair of saddle shoes. While I would freeze, my mouth gaping like a lunatic, like a slow-witted sidekick. Until in the end that is all I became: her silent accomplice, her cover as she sought out new thrills, new worlds, and no longer needed ours.

But with Penn, it could be different. It *will* be different.

"To town, Mrs Pennington?" he says.

It's a joke, I know. But with those words, I feel surety fill me with treacle warmth. "To town," I say, smiling. Then I laugh, my head thrown back with the thrill of it. "To town!"

Like the creek, Calenick changes with the seasons. Steep streets of tightly packed houses, clinging to each other and to the rock like limpets or stubborn barnacles. In the winter they glower, staring grimly out at a sea that is as grey as their own granite walls. But in the summer they dress up, wink brazenly, their faces decked with bunting as crowds of tourists throng the pavements, queue for ice cream or a cone of hot, salty chips or the mackerel boats that they can write home about, boasting about their catch, claiming they are a natural.

The older I got the less I liked summer in Calenick. As my taste for ice lollies or polystyrene pots of prawns waned, so did my tolerance of crowds; of braying boys and horse-faced girls. I felt out of place, out of time – the boat girl in her outdated dress and school plimsolls.

But today is different. Today I'm full of pride, of power. His arm through mine is a shield, a shining cloak that reflects back the confidence of these strangers as swiftly as it sweeps away the pity of those I know: the silver-haired, bent-backed Mrs Cardew; John Penrice in his Land Rover; the vicar, hot under his dog collar.

We walk into the Lugger. Into the orange-soaked dimness and stale taint of beer.

"But I'm not eighteen," I say. "Not for weeks yet."

"He doesn't know that," Penn replies, nodding towards the bar.

I look at the bartender, his hair sun-bleached and long, his accent from far away – Australia or New Zealand. He doesn't know me. Penn is right. He doesn't know me at all. None of them do, not really, not today. Today I'm different: bright, brilliant. I'm the kind of girl to whom people pay attention; the kind who lets herself be bought lobster knowing he can pay for it; the kind who washes it down with vodka and tonic, then another, and another. So that by the time we walk back down the steps to the street I'm giddy; with alcohol, with freedom, with Penn.

So giddy my shoulder crashes into an oncomer from the throng, making me stumble, lose my grip on Penn. I have to reach to the wall to steady myself, laughing.

I look up, and my eyes meet my assailant's.

It's Tom.

I wait for it, for the accusations, the reprimands, the

pleas. But he says nothing. Just looks at me. His eyes move up and down, taking me in. The newness of me, the difference. He looks at me the way I wanted him to look last summer; like I'm worth having, like I am the prize, as he was mine. "Well it's too late," I tell him silently as I loop my arm back through Penn's. "I don't want you any more. I don't need you any more."

And I don't. Whatever I felt for Tom pales when I see him next to Penn. Tom and I are done, we are over. If we ever really began.

"Who was that?" Penn asks, turning.

I watch Tom's back as he weaves his way up Ship Street. "Nobody," I say.

I tug at his arm. "Come on."

"Where to now, my lady?"

The grey, gated church is to our right. I had planned on showing him her grave. So he could say what he would have said at the funeral. So he could say goodbye. But…

"She's not there, is she? Not really."

I shake my head.

"She's at Eden," he says, saying the words for me. "The real Bea. She's at home."

"Yes, home," I say. "Take me home."

And so he does. He drives slower this time, more sedately. For we are grown-ups, not children playing any more.

Back up the hill to the edge of the village.

Back down the narrow road that winds through the woods.

Back to Eden.

Back to Bea.

JUNE 1988

SHE FINDS *him last. The sound of the door being flung open startles him. It's been half an hour, maybe more since he crept in, and sleep crept up, as he waited, waited.*

But she's not alone. And she isn't staying.

"You're 'it'," she says triumphantly. Just two words, then dances off, a Greek chorus of punch-drunk Pans in her wake, but no Penn, for Penn has refused to play, says he's not in the mood for games today.

James doesn't want to play any more either. Instead he will play a trick, he thinks. He will let them hide away, bury themselves in corners and cupboards, then he, the Great James, Master of Mysteries, will disappear. And after, when she has sat alone in the dark, counting down the minutes and hours, she'll know what it is to wait for someone.

And so he creeps carefully, quickly down the stairs, his feet noiseless on the carpet. He's good at this, has had years of practice at home – walking on eggshells around Theresa and Brigid once a month, tiptoeing past his da and Deirdre every Saturday night to wash off the smell of sweat and smoke and sin.

He's at the bottom of the stairs now. The front door is just ahead. He'll slip outside and then his vanishing trick will be complete. But then he hears a sound from Penn's room: a suppressed giggle, then another voice – a man's – speaks low, then groans. They're in there together – him and Bea. They're not playing by the rules. He hesitates. The door is ajar, a sliver of light from a lava lamp playing on the tiles. He knows he shouldn't, that this isn't some Berwick Street peepshow. But the need to know what is happening is overwhelming, and so he presses his face against the jamb, and peers in.

It takes him a few seconds for his eyes to focus in the half-light, and two or three more for them to register what he's seeing. Then he has to suppress a sharp intake of breath, a gasp out. For it's worse than he imagined. And better too, so much better.

Because there is Penn; his wet, desperate lips on her face, his hand inside the cream chiffon of her top. And there is the girl, her fingers on the swell of his crotch.

And James smiles, because he's found it, he's found the weakness. And this time it isn't just a chink, but a huge gaping hole.

Because the girl Penn is kissing isn't Bea.

It's Stella.

AUGUST 1988

THE HOUSE is empty when we return. The decorators
have gone for the day, their paint brushes leaving milky
trails on the kitchen drainer. On the table is a note from
Tom's mum Hannah: "Come to dinner, we miss you."

"Do you want to?" Penn asks me.

I shake my head. "Too full still." But it's not that. I don't
want to go, alone or with him. Don't want anyone to prick
this bubble of perfection.

And nor does he, I'm sure of it.

"We'll have a party of our own," he says abruptly. "A
cocktail party. We'll have crisps, and peanuts in glass
bowls. And we can dress up."

"In what?" I ask.

"You have dresses, don't you?"

I shrug awkwardly. I don't any more.

I did once: Bea's hand-me-downs, velvet things with lace collars, then later, drop-waisted, or with net skirts swishing round my thighs. They were always a year or two out of date, but I didn't mind, for in them I was her. Or almost. But then she grew taller, grew breasts, and I couldn't catch up, so she either kept her clothes for herself or they were sent to charity. And now I live in T-shirts, leggings; a black uniform of "don't-look-at-me".

But Penn has other ideas. "Come with me," he says. And this time, it is he who leads me up the stairs.

I wonder what he's brought with him. If he has a coat of many colours or a Cinderella outfit hidden away in his bag upstairs.

But it's not his treasure he is plundering, it's mine. Ours.

We're standing in front of the door to Narnia: my grand-parents' wardrobe, leading not to snow-capped mountains or forests thick with fir, but to furs. And to black-beaded dresses that tickle my toes with their jet bugles; to pink silk slips that drape across the flesh like liquid skin; to gold brocade gowns whose opulence begs to be chosen, jostling, "pick me, pick me!"

I've stood in front of that wardrobe before, with Bea; our eyes wide, as if we were looking on sweet jars full of gobstoppers and candy canes. She would take armfuls of dresses down, parade in them in turn, catwalking across the carpet in too-big heels while I, on the bed, clapped and whistled, a child still in my Ladybird sundress and flip-flops. It wasn't that I didn't dare try on the clothes. Rather, why would I bother? When I could watch her, when she was the one they were made for, really.

But not tonight. Tonight is different.

"Which one?" I ask.

"That's up to you," he says. "Who do you want to be?"

"Who do you want me to be?" I ask quickly. Because I'll be anyone, will play any part, for him.

But he shakes his head. "You don't get it, do you? You," he says. "I want you to be you."

The invitation is for seven-thirty. I'm to meet him in the drawing room, where he'll be waiting to escort me, in a grey suit belonging to my grandfather.

Until then I stand in front of my mirror, take in the girl I have become: the lips painted a heavy, sticky red; the eyes ringed with black kohl; the hair pinned up on my head in a dishevelled bun. And the dress: a 1950s emerald shot taffeta, like the hard shiny shell of a beetle, glimmering with blues and yellows as I move, its skirt rustling in anticipation.

"I want you to be you," he said.

But I don't want to play me. Me is shy. Me is awkward; all bones and too-skinny legs. Me doesn't wear stockings, or gold rings, or pearls around her throat.

But look: this me does.

This me wears heels.

This me walks, bold as Bea, brave as Bea, down the staircase, one gloved hand on the banister, the diamonds in my cuff catching in the light of the glass chandelier.

This me takes his arm, and doesn't blush or giggle when he says, "Why, Mrs Pennington, you look beautiful tonight."

This me simply smiles, and says, "Why, thank you, darling." And lets him sweep her to the excitement that awaits.

He's transformed again; a 1940s cad in a demob suit, his pale hair dark with the slick of brilliantine. He puts on music, slips a cassette into the player he rescued from the boathouse, presses play, says, "Would you care to dance?"

And this girl does, she does care. "I would love to dance," she replies.

And she – no longer the schoolgirl in the hall, her arm clamped around Monica Coyne as they stamp out another waltz to Mrs Bonnet's lamentable piano – she glides now, elegant in his arms, as Morrissey sings a slow, sad love song, tells her the light will never go out.

They move in time, as one, their steps almost indistinguishable, the line between them blurred.

"We're Bonnie and Clyde," he says in her ear.

And he is right, for this couple is fugitive from their other selves.

"Bonnie and Clyde," she repeats. Then adds, "Superman and Lois Lane."

"Romeo and Juliet," he completes. "You and me against the world."

She feels him pull her tighter to him, feels his heart against hers; lower, feels his want, his need.

"You do believe that, don't you?" he asks urgently, his words tangling in her hair, winding around her ear.

She nods, her head rubbing against his cheek.

And then it happens.

He slows the turn of their dance to a halt, lifts her head, her chin cupped in his hand, and, like Rhett Butler, like Romeo, he kisses her.

And though they are still now, she feels the room spinning, a dizzy giddy dance, and they are at the centre of it all. She is breathless, swooning, almost, and in that moment she realizes she does not care if it is truly her he is kissing, or the gone girl, the girl before.

She only wants for it never to stop.

JULY 1988

WHEN PENN *wakes, he feels the crackle of condom wrapper beneath his skin and finds himself checking, like he used to. Who is she? Is she still here? But Bea is in her room, her door locked before the party was even over, and Stella, she is long gone back to Nunhead.*

"It's not my fault," he says to himself to see off the guilt that threatens to consume him. "I was drunk, it was nothing, it won't happen again."

But by the next day he is squaring his conscience with alarming ease, dismissing Bea as if she were no more than a bothersome child, blaming her. She's losing interest anyway, he thinks. She's always wrapped up in some production or other, or private drama of her own making. But Stella isn't too busy. Stella adores him. She hangs on his every word and actually cries when he mentions his father, who has only months, maybe weeks to live.

So lost in this game of deceit is he, he doesn't see that someone else is playing along too.

For two days James keeps the secret, holds it close: a bright diamond hidden in his tight fist. But the exhilaration of knowing becomes unbearable, and the white-hot jewel begins to burn his skin.

He sees the girl – Stella – in the refectory on Monday. A pathetic thing: obvious in her blondeness, in her cultivated fragility. He watches as she sits opposite Penn, brazenly pushes her foot against his while Bea chews methodically on a sandwich, engrossed in a script, oblivious to her all-too-public humiliation.

On Thursday Penn misses a meeting, and Bea confronts him later in the studio in front of everyone. She demands to know where he's been. Penn mumbles something about a solicitor, apologizes, cups her chin and kisses her, filling her with promises he cannot keep.

And James can stand it no longer.

The next day he finds Bea at the noticeboard in the theatre stairwell; she is looking for a message from Penn, fingering each slip of paper in turn, in the hope it will be for her.

"Hey," he says.

She turns, startled. When she sees it is him, she doesn't

bother to hide the disappointment in her "Oh, hi."

"I need to talk to you."

"Not now." She turns back to the board.

"Yes, now." He takes her hand and pulls her into a dressing room, sits her on the table so that she is backlit by a hundred bright bulbs; a star, the one and only. She doesn't deserve to be treated like this by Penn and she doesn't deserve what he's going to tell her, but he has to tell her.

"I saw him," he says.

"Saw who?" she is flippant, impatient, eyes flicking to the door in case he comes for her after all.

"Penn."

"What? Now?" She checks the door again, confused.

"No." A coal of anger fuels the fire that she could be so bound to Penn, so beholden to a fool. And any shred of conflict over what he is about to do is gone. Because yes, what he is about to say will break her. But then he, the true hero, will pick her up, carry her home, heal her, be there for her, as he has been every day since he first saw her.

"Not now," he continues. "At the party. He— he was with someone, Bea."

She looks blankly at him, still angry, still confused.

"Jesus, he was kissing someone else." Then he softens again. He cannot be the villain; that is Penn, has to be Penn. "I'm so sorry." He pulls her into his chest.

And then it crystallizes, what he's telling her, and her hands slam against his shoulders, pushing him sharply away.

"No," she says. "I don't believe you." But doubt is etched

on her face, contorting it. Because she knows he is capable, knows his reputation.

"Who then?" she sneers. "Go on, who?"

"Stella. Stella French." As if it could be another.

There is silence, enough for four heartbeats. And then, "You're lying," she says.

"No, I—"

"You're jealous. You've always been jealous."

"Of him?"

"Yes. Because everyone loves him... Because I love him."

He looks away so she can't see that she has found a truth, or half-truth, because he does covet what Penn has. But he doesn't want to be Penn; would rather be anyone than that cheat, that liar, that poor little rich boy.

He lifts his head up again, emboldened by the thought. "You deserve better."

"What, like you?" she snaps.

He says nothing. Lets her throw sticks and stones, a volley of accusations and insults. Because she doesn't mean them. Can't mean them. You always hurt those closest to you, don't you? That's what his ma used to say about his da. He doesn't mean it, he loves you really. It's only when Bea snatches her bag off the floor that he lets himself speak.

"Where are you going?" he demands.

"Away from you."

And she turns and slams the door behind her, and he's left staring at the space where she had been, so that all he can see is an infinite number of Jameses reflected in this hall of *mirrors. And they all wear the same face: a smile, a Cheshire-cat-that-got-the-cream grin. For despite her denials, despite her accusations and protestations, he knows he has won. Penn and Bea cannot survive this, and then she will be his.*

For the first time in a long time, he walks tall; elated, amplified by this power. He is cloaked in it, a great, technicolour thing.

He has felt this triumph before; this rising, like a bright bird from the shadows. He was the hero then, too. But the villain was played not by Penn, nor even another boy, but by his own da.

He bought the coat from Affleck's Palace in Manchester; an Aladdin's cave of discarded velveteen and dead men's shoes, hung with the beguiling mix of patchouli and their long-departed owners. He'd seen it in the window on a meandering, time-wasting walk to the station and saved for four long weeks to afford it. Four weeks of Saturdays in the sweaty, yeasty heat of the bakery, and Sundays in the backroom of Grimshaw's, sorting papers for delivery: the heavy, frowning sobriety of broadsheets for Mesnes Park; the wide-mawed, finger-wagging red tops for the terraces, his own amongst their number. But he was neither. He was more. And the coat was the start of it.

The coat was dark brown suede, like the skin of a pony, and lined with silk paisley in startling reds and emeralds. And long – so long it threatened to graze the gum-spattered pavement, but then would rise miraculously with each dancing step. It was a dreamcoat. And inside it, he was Joseph, the prodigal son.

His sisters said nothing when they saw it. For once their screeching aviary-like chatter was silenced, but their disdain was clear: Siobhan let her mouth gape open, a wodge of Hubba Bubba nestled pinkly on her tongue; Brigid signalled hers with a single, incredulous snort.

But his da had something to say. His da always had something to say.

"What the bleedin' hell do you think you look like?" he demanded.

Seamus looked down at himself in his finery, then back at the man in front of him, a red-faced mass in a yellowing vest and trousers held up by a piece of twine since the belt buckle gave way. I look like a prince, he thought, a king. Compared to you.

"He looks like a poof," declared Deirdre.

Brigid went one better. "He looks like Mental Davey."

"Mental Davey," chanted Brigid, her head bobbing from side to side. "Mental Davey, Mental Davey."

Siobhan joined in, buoyed both by Brigid's daring and the sheer audacity of her brother. "Mental Davey, Mental Davey," she repeated with delight. Because the coat was a joke. It had to be. No one dared to wear a coat like that in real life. Not round here.

No one except Seamus.

But their da wasn't laughing. He was staring, disgust contorting his flaccid features.

"That's enough." He slammed his hand down on the worktop, sending Siobhan's plastic beaker of Ribena skittering over the Formica, a pool of purple inching incrementally towards the edge.

The first drop of juice plopped satisfactorily onto the linoleum, but no one moved to mop it up. No one dared. The air was dense, the room heaving with possibility.

Another drop.

And then it broke.

He stood. "Outside. Now," he said.

They went to the bottom of the garden. Just him and his da. The women shut in the house where they couldn't scream or scold or stop him. Not that they'd try, Seamus thought.

"Take it off," his da commanded.

He had toyed with resisting, with uttering a single defiant "No". But his da had a foot and twenty-eight pounds on him; a bulk and temper that had once floored Garv O'Riley down the John Bull with two sharp jabs, one to the stomach, one to the head. Seamus was no match for that. Not even in his coat.

Seamus slipped the garment off his shoulders and let it drop to the ground at his feet.

And so it was his da who picked it up and dropped it in the brazier on top of the dead leaves and yesterday's news, as if it were no more than a broken toy, an outgrown, worn-out thing.

But it was more than that. It was the end and beginning of it all.

"You know why I'm doing this, son?" said his da.

Seamus knew why. But he said nothing. He had long since learned that silence was the easier option. The only option, if you valued your skin.

His da didn't wait for an answer anyway. "It's for your own good. You'll thank me one day."

But Seamus wouldn't. He knew it then, even at the age of seventeen, that he would thank this hulking sack of ignorance and hatred for nothing. This working-class villain with his sex on a Saturday and church on Sunday. His life undistinguished, his soul untouched by ambition. Any treasure, any glimmer of brilliance, any hope of something more that shone in Seamus came from his ma. And she was gone. And soon he would be too.

He could smell the petrol from the brazier now, its choking fumes seeping into the suede, staining it darker, sleeker, turning the lining from ruby to blood red.

"I don't know what you're smiling at," said his da.

But Seamus couldn't stop. Because it was funny, laughable. Because he didn't need the coat. Because where he was going there were other coats, brighter, more fabulous, more powerful. Because it wasn't the coat that burned bright anyway. It was him. He was on fire, cleansed, purified.

The flames swallowed the fabric, but his flesh was intact. Out of the ashes James rose like a phoenix. Clean. New. Strong.

AUGUST 1988

BEA AND I had imagined what it would be like – to go to bed with a man; to wake up beside him the next morning. We'd pulled faces and vowed we never would; cited their stupidity, their animal hairiness, their bestial smell as reasons. And yet, just two years later, she'd already done that three times and I knew from her whispered conversations on the phone and louder ones in the toilets at school that she planned on doing it a lot more. But I was scared to finish anything I started. So I ran away from Rory Ellis after I let him kiss me behind the Lugger one night, his tongue poking wetly into my mouth like the eels we watched writhing in buckets on the dock. And ran away from Tom a year later.

And yet, as I awake that morning, Penn's bare body just inches from mine, the taste of him still on my tongue, the feel of him still on my skin, I understand, finally I understand. I watch as the sun dapples across his back, catches the edges of a tattoo on his shoulder – a bird ringed by fire – and I imagine his bravery to suffer the needle digging in and out of his flesh to carve the feathers and the flames, and then imagine the scene when his mother saw the result.

The house is silent still. It's a Saturday and there are no workers today, so there's no one to disturb us. Not even her. She's quiet now; there's nothing left for her to say, not a whisper. For it's done. I love him, just as she did, as much as she did. And he loves me.

He stirs, stretches languidly, cat-like, then turns to me, pulls me to him. And so it begins again.

"What do you want to be when you grow up?" he asks me.

"I am grown up," I say. "I'm not a child."

He laughs. "I didn't mean that. I'm sorry."

And I feel the irritation pop and dissipate, like a tiny bubble; laugh with him. "I don't know," I say. For I can't repeat my childhood answer; can't tell him what I told my grandparents, teachers, Tom. Then, thinking, remembering something Bea said: "I want to read the complete works of Shakespeare," I say. "I want to understand jazz, I want to fall in love with an older man."

"So just two to go, then."

I smile. "What about you?"

"I don't ever want to grow up," he says. "When you grow up your heart dies. You stop caring about beauty and poetry and music, and start buying *The Sun* and saving for holidays in Benidorm. I'm going to stay young for ever." And it's not a wish, but a promise.

"Like Peter Pan," I say.

"Just like Pan."

The sun is high in the sky now. Half the day is gone already, half this wondrous, precious, perfect day. We have moved little from the bed, only to fetch water, some fruit or to open the windows wide to let in air. The smell of summer grass, and salt winds, and something else now, something unpleasant, rough, fills the room.

"What is that?" he asks. "That smell."

"Smoke," I say. "They're burning the fields."

I have come to hate that smell, not just for the eye-stinging smog that imprisons you in the house for a day, or the charred black slivers of corn stem that flit through open doors, stick to your lotion-sticky skin, but because it signifies summer's end. The end of Eden. Mixed up in the burning vegetation is the smell of school; of overboiled vegetables, of the beeswax on the gymnasium floor, of the unfamiliar soap and hairspray of nine other girls in beds next to mine, none of them Bea.

"I lied," I say, suddenly. "When I said that thing about Shakespeare, that wasn't true. Well, I mean I do want to read them, but not just that."

"So you do have a burning ambition," he smiles. "I knew it."

"Not— not in the normal way," I stammer. I am unsure how to tell him, what to tell him.

"What do you mean?"

And then it comes out, because I cannot physically keep it in any longer. Because time is running out. The decorators are nearly done and then Aunt Julia will be back. "I don't want to go," I say. "That's it. When I grow up I don't want to be an actress or anything like that. I just want to stay here. At Eden."

I wait for the laugh, the roll of eyes, or the "I don't think you get it." But they don't come. Instead he sits up, pulls me with him, says just two words:

"Then stay."

I don't understand. "But it's decided," I tell him. "The house is for sale. I'm going back to school, then to Aunt Julia's at Christmas."

"Did you decide?"

"Well, no—"

"Then it doesn't have to happen." He speaks with precision and determination. He is someone else; is his father, I think, the public speaker, the man who made things happen, who stopped them. "The house is half yours, right?"

"Yes, but—"

"But nothing. You want to stay, yeah?"

"Yes?"

"Then we'll stay."

"Both of us?"

"You and me against the world, remember."

I nod. "But how?"

"Watch."

And I do. I watch as he stops time in its tracks. As he pulls dustsheets off furniture in a triumphant "ta-dah!" And there, underneath, are gleaming tables, soft velvet chairs that smile blinking in the sun. I watch as he stacks paint pots and white spirit in the outhouse, hauls rolls of wallpaper, brushes a pair of overalls into a pile on the gravel. "We'll burn them," he says. "It's not just an end though. A new beginning. The start of us."

And so we burn it all; a spilling, toppling bonfire in an old dustbin. I think of Bea. This fire should scare me, send me scuttling back into my torpor, into that strange, lost state of wandering without my Wendy. But now, with Pan beside me, everything is different.

"You feel it, don't you?" he says.

And I do. The searing heat scalds my fingers and the flames dance in my eyes. They are purging us. All the old, the bad things, are being destroyed, rendered nothing but ashes and air. And so they can't harm me now. No one can harm me now. No one can take me away from Eden. The phone has been unplugged, the gates closed, the key to the padlock buried deep in the back of a drawer; a sign to the world that we will not leave. And they can't come in. Only if they dare brave the river and the woods and only Tom has ever done that. But this new, unstoppable, invincible me can handle Tom. Now that I no longer want him, need him, love him. I am Penn's now, and he is mine. "You and me against the world." We are all we need.

And so, the last furls of smoke curling into the fading afternoon sky, hand-in-hand we walk into Eden, close the doors on the world; on danger, on badness, on change.

So happy, so high am I that I don't think to check what, who, I have locked in.

JULY 1988

IT'S TWO *days before Bea can face Penn. Two days of sleeping on the floor at Hetty's; of eating cereal from the packet and watching endless, mindless television.*

"You have to go home," Hetty says when she gets home from the bar to find Bea staring at white noise in a sea of Sugar Puffs. "You have to talk to him."

And so, at two in the morning, Bea walks slowly, steadily up Telegraph Hill.

He's awake when she finds him, halfway-through-a-bottle-of-whisky drunk, lying bare-chested on his bed. His hair needs a wash; the sheets too. Bea wonders who else has left their mark on there and feels a surge of nausea so strong that she has to hold her breath and clench her fists to push it down. But she won't cry. She won't give him the satisfaction.

"Babe," he says. "Want a drink?" He takes a swig from the bottle and then holds it out to her.

She shakes her head. "Is it true?" she asks.

He takes another swig. "Is what true?"

"You and—" She cannot say her name. "… that girl."

"You'll have to be more specific." He raises the bottle to his lips but Bea snatches it away, drops it onto the floor where it seeps its brown contents in a widening pool.

"Jesus, Bea. What the fuck?"

"Did you sleep with her?"

"With who?"

She balls her fists again, musters the strength to spit the name out. "Stella French."

He stares at her, incredulous. And she waits for the denial. Of course he'll refute it. He'll tell her she's imagining things and is a fool for listening to gossip, for listening to James. She wants him to tell her that it's jealousy, that's all, the green-eyed monster. James is trying to stir things so he can have her to himself.

But instead he drops his eyes and says a single life-changing, heartbreaking word.

He says, "Yes."

Bea claps a hand over her mouth, a fake gesture she thinks, one she's been warned off by tutors on stage. But here, in real life, her hand flies to her face without thinking, as if to keep something in: her words, or tears, or anger.

"Babe." He tries to grasp her free hand but she snatches it away.

"Don't touch me."

"Bea, don't be like this. I was drunk, and upset and you—you were gone."

"Oh, so it's my fault, is it?"

"I didn't say that."

He paused. "It didn't mean anything. She doesn't mean anything to me."

"Yeah? But nor did I. Not when you were screwing her. I meant nothing to you then."

"Bea, you need to calm down. You're overreacting."

"Fuck you." She picks up the bottle and throws it against the wall, where it smashes and drops behind the headboard, a shower of glass and liquor raining down on the pillows.

"Bea, pack it in."

But she won't. She picks up a shoe and hurls it straight at Penn this time. He ducks, but she's a good shot. She learned from Evie how to catapult, how to bowl a tennis ball, and it glances off his shoulder.

"Fuck's sake. That hurt."

"Good," she snaps. "Now you know how I feel."

She looks around for more ammunition, so that she can beat it out of him, out of her. But Penn is wired now, adrenalin drowning out the whisky, and he grabs her, pulls her to him and her struggle lasts only seconds before she collapses into him.

"You're the one," he says. "It's always been you."

"I don't believe you," she sobs.

"But you have to." He is shaking her by the shoulders now. "You have to."

She stares at him, at this boy she loves, at this boy she believed was the one, too. Who she thought would end, erase all that had gone before. But what if she was wrong? What if she chose the wrong boy? What if—

"Let go," she says.

"Bea—"

"I said let go."

"You can't leave. I have to go to Hampshire in the morning. I need you with me. I need—"

"I don't care what you need any more."

"That's not true."

"Isn't it? Because you know me so well? Yeah? Well, you're not the only one." James knows me, she thinks. He knows me better even.

She turns to leave.

"Where are you going?"

"What does it matter?"

"Are you going to Hetty's?"

"Yeah," she lies. "I'm going to Hetty's."

But when she gets to the bottom of the hill, it's not left she turns to Peckham, but right. Right towards the Old Kent Road, and right towards a bedsit above a kebab shop with a cooker in the corner and a bathroom down the hall.

Right towards James.

AUGUST 1988

FOR THREE days we hold on. Three days in our own small paradise. Three days of sleeping late, past the song of blackbirds, past the distant hum of motorboats, and the call of the ferry, until the sun had begun its slow descent to earth again. Three days of lying, curled in our still-damp sheets, or in the hot, foggy steam of the bath, listening to him read Keats and Yeats, explaining the world, explaining us. Three days of dancing in the drawing room to our stack of battered tapes; with wild, reckless abandon to Joy Division and The Wedding Present, then slow, melting waltzes to the sorrowful sound of the Smiths.

Without heating the house becomes cold once more. Shivering, he lights me a fire and we lie naked in front of it, the skin on our chests and thighs as red and raw as my heart. My love for him is a fever. When he says jump, I jump. If he asked me to die for him I would plunge the knife in a thousand times over. With him I'm safe, with him anything is possible, achievable.

The world tries to get in. It rattles at the gates and tries to slip sideways through the railings. The decorators leave a note on the gate's padlock, asking what's going on, saying they need paying, and they want their things back. Tom comes too. He actually makes it to the back door; hammers on the window, so hard that I go and see him for fear he will break the glass.

"What are you doing?" he rages.

I pull Penn's cardigan tighter around me. "Living," I say, calmly.

"Julia will go crazy, you know that."

"I don't care," I say. And I mean it.

He turns to go, then changes his mind, comes back for one last try. "I don't recognize you any more," he says. "You've changed. You're like, like—"

"Say it, go on. I'm like Bea. That's what you mean, isn't it? I thought that was who you wanted?"

He shakes his head, laughs, a guttural sound, scornful. "I wanted you. I told you. I wanted you but you said no, and she was the closest I could get."

My heart teeters for a second on the brink of something. But I do not let it fall. At the last moment, I pull it back tighter into me, into Penn.

"You know she laughed at you," I sneer. "That time. She never wanted you. You were nothing to her." I'm on fire now, lit by Penn, my flames fanned by his love, his belief in me. "And this— this is me, I'm me. Not anyone else. You hear me?"

But he doesn't. I'm talking to an empty space. Tom has gone, disappeared back into the woods. As if by magic.

And then Penn comes into the kitchen. He wraps his arms around me, holds me, and my fleeting doubt is over. The outside has tried its best, sent its bravest, cleverest soldiers, but no one can breach our barricades. Nothing can touch us in here.

Then, on the fourth morning I wake early, shaken from a bad dream of a terrible claustrophobia of walls closing in on me. And a memory is sparked, of Bea reading Milton in her last summer here, her head lost in the poetry. Then another memory comes to me, of Sunday school as a child of five.

I feel a lurch of nausea rise in me, tugged up like mud on roots. For I remember the stories now. Remember how it happens. That Paradise was lost in the end. Eden did fall. But it wasn't plundered or pillaged from neighbouring lands or far-flung fiefdoms. Rather, it was destroyed by itself, ruined from the inside. And I realize that what we have isn't sustainable. Despite the gates and the locks and the shutters, the world is closing in. Like the damp that's returned to the pantry, rot is creeping into Eden. And I don't know how to stop it.

JULY 1988

SHE COMES *to him. Of course she does.*

James wakes at gone three to the sound of a desperate finger pressed against the doorbell. Wordlessly, he lets her in and then lets her curl up on his faded Superman duvet while he sits at the end of the bed and watches her sleep, his tattooed back against the wall, his soul open, waiting.

Then, when she wakes, he listens as she tells him that Penn didn't even bother to deny it. Just dismissed the infidelity, like he was waving away a moth. It meant nothing, he said. She was the one, she must know that.

"Do you believe him?" he asks.

Her head is hung low with shame and sorrow and her fingers worry at a pulled thread. She looks up at him, meets his eyes, says steadily, truthfully, "I don't know what I believe any more."

And he knows he's won. She'll never trust Penn again now, but he, James, has never lied to her, never deceived her, never cheated her. She'll see him now for what he is: clean and pure and true. And worthy of her, even without money and a house in the country and the title to come. And their little world will be perfect, for they won't need much, just each other.

Just him and Bea against it all. Him and Bea against the world.

AUGUST 1988

THE SIGNS are there, the clues. Like a trail of bread-crumbs laid before me. In the months, years, to come, I will see them clearly; white morsels against the dark woods. But now … now all I see is him.

I have built a future with him in my head, woven a fiction of weddings and children and death do us part. I give him a silver box that had once belonged to my grand-mother, worth hundreds, I know.

"I can't," he says.

"Please. I want you to have it."

"But I've got nothing to give you. No heirlooms."

"What did your father leave you?" I ask.

"A broken heart," he says. "And bad memories.

Whatever good things, precious things I had, he destroyed them."

Sorrow wells in me, the swell of an orchestra in a minor key.

"It doesn't matter," he says, cutting the chords short. "None of them matter. You're my family now."

Then he sees something, plucks it like a diamond from dark tarmac. "You know what we should do?"

I shake my head, eager for his latest plan, his latest trick.

"Write wills," he says. "So we know that all of us goes to the other, when we die. That no one can take anything from us."

"Yes," I say, testing the idea. Then surer. "Yes, we must."

And so we do. We find the typewriter in a tea chest, dust off its keys like black buttons, reset the ribbon, load it with thick vellum the colour and richness of clotted cream. Then together, one-fingered and laughing with each clack and each inky letter imprinting, we write a contract to our love.

To me he leaves his worldly possessions: his clothes, his books, his badges. And more precious things too: the thoughts in his head, the light of the sun, the "Song to the Siren".

To him I bequeath a beetle, bright and shining that crawled across the sheets one morning and lives now in a shoe box in the lounge. But more: I give him my heart, my soul. And Eden. Eden is to be his.

And then we sign our names at the bottom. He goes first, trailing the fountain pen across the ridges in the snaking loop of a J. Then he stops and looks at what he has done, and I see a brief flicker of confusion. But just as quickly, it is gone, and with bold strokes he finishes with a flourish: "James Dean" it reads.

I laugh, and sign my own: Marilyn Monroe.

But as the days pass he becomes agitated. As though, while I shiver in the cold granite walls, he burns, is on fire. He's taken to climbing on the roof and reaching over the parapet, his arms flung open as if he's the figurehead on a ship, as if he is flying. "I'm king of the world!" he screams into the wind. "The creek, the trees, the sea. It's all mine. This whole world is mine."

His, not ours, I think.

And I feel a tiny crack open up in the plaster of our life. Its jagged black hairline runs through the pristine pale pink of the palace we have built.

And someone else sees it too. For Bea is back, flown through the gap in an air brick, or the roof-hatch when he has gone out to survey his lands. And now she dances, moth-like, in and out of rooms, following me, taunting me. *Be careful, Evie. Be careful who you love.*

Then, one afternoon as I wait for him to come down, I see on the window sill what I think is a dead bee, its wings a shimmering, clear lace, its furred body soft, touchable. But when I pick it up it shudders and I feel a red-hot needle stab into the pad of my forefinger. Gasping, I drop it, then pull out the sharp, black stinger. But it is too late, I am hurt, and the bee is dead.

He finds me in the bathroom, my throbbing hand under the cold tap.

"What happened?" he asks.

"I pricked it on a needle," I lie. "Stupid really." Because I can't tell him the truth. That this small hurt is just a warning of bigger ones to come. That I think Bea is telling me to stop trusting him, believing in him – in us.

He takes my hand from the sink, kisses each wet, freezing finger in turn. "All better now. Nothing can hurt you now. I'll protect you."

But the truth pulses through me like the insect's poison. Bea is dead and I have stolen her boyfriend for my own. It can't last. This Eden can't last. "What about Julia?" I want to say. "What will you say to her? What about your mother? What's going to happen to us?"

But, "Come to bed," he says.

And I do. I slip between sheets and close my eyes to the fractures. So the next morning our paradise is papered over again. It is fresh and new and full of the possibility of perfection.

But by that evening a criss-cross of faults has appeared: minute changes in his accent; his refusal to talk about his family when I have bared all about mine; why he hitched – why not bring his MG? – he has money for petrol after all; he's not broke, far from it.

"What does that matter now?" he demands. "We don't need it. We're not leaving."

"Well, at some point—" I begin.

But that point hasn't occurred to him, will not be acknowledged.

"I thought you understood me, Evie. I thought you believed in me. I'm here to protect you. You don't need anyone else. This is it now. Me and you. Just me and you."

And he holds me by the wrists so tightly, the pain squeezing tears from my eyes, that I can do nothing but nod, agree with him, tell him of course I believe him, of course he is right. I don't need anyone. Don't want anyone.

Until, one day, something happens that tears a rent in the fabric so wide and severe that it cannot be sewn up.

And who wielded the knife?

Tom, of course. Who else but Tom?

JULY 1988

SHE STAYS *for three days. For three days she is his, and his alone.*

Days that pass with the blind pulled down against the light, against Penn, against the world. Of eating only what they can scavenge from the back of the cupboard and the bottom of the biscuit tin. Of talking until they can hear the soft, steady rumble of the night buses give way to vans, lorries, taxis, and the swelling, impatient flow of commuters into town. Of lying in silent, dazed wonder at what they have, what they have done.

Then, one evening he wakes and the room is cold and dark. The covers have been pulled back and the sun has already sunk behind the gas tower so that he knows it is late, gone five. He reaches across the sheets for her, but the bed is empty. Instead she is sitting at the window. But something in the atmosphere has changed, shifted. She is dressed now, with a cardigan pulled around her like a cocoon, hair pulled back in an elastic band.

"Hey," he says. "Come back to bed?"

But she doesn't answer. Instead she looks down, and in that instant he sees what has happened. Because there, in her lap, is a letter, two white sheets of looped, childish cursive, and an envelope addressed to a lost boy, a boy she doesn't know.

"Who's Brigid?" she asks.

"I—"

"Actually, no. More to the point, who's Seamus?" Each word is heavy, bitter.

"It's a long story."

"It would be. Christ, I don't even know who you are – who I've been with... How could you? How could you lie to me?"

"I wasn't lying— I'm not lying," he pleads. "I'm James. I just changed my name. That's all. Just my name." But he knows this is an untruth. That Seamus is gone. That he is new. The thoughts are coming hard and fast, the panic rising, battering inside his chest. He will tell her, tell her everything, he thinks. Tell her about da, and Deirdre, about his ma who told him he would fly to the sun.

"Don't. Don't bother. It doesn't matter anyway now."

Oh God, she's going, he thinks. She's leaving me. He stands then, his naked body exposed, vulnerable. "Please.

Please don't go." He drops to the floor, scrabbles for his things, pulls on a T-shirt. "Is it clothes you need? I'll get clothes for you. I'll go back to the house. What else do you want? Do you want the mirror? We can put it here, on the desk." He pushes aside books and papers, sending them scattering across the boards.

"What are you doing?" She is looking at him oddly. She doesn't understand.

"Moving you in. You can live here. With me," he adds, as if this part is unclear.

"No." She says it quietly. So that maybe it means a yes, he thinks.

"It'll be perfect. You'll see. I can do anything," he says. Then corrects himself; "I can do everything."

"No." This one is louder. Definitive.

"But you have to. Please," he begs, grabbing her shoulders in his hands.

She pulls back. "Stop it. You're scaring me."

Then it hits him. And he wants to laugh. And cry. "You're going back to Penn."

"Jesus. No. He's not there, I told you. No one is. He's in Hampshire. And the others, I don't know. Home, I guess."

"But you'll be alone. You can't be alone."

"Yes... No— I... I'm not staying. I'm going back. I need to go back."

"Go back where?"

"Eden," she says. "I'm going home."

"But, but... " His mind is racing with reasons, excuses.

"Term's not over," he blurts. "And the house is being sold."

"Still, I—"

"And Evie!" He grasps her name from the air like it is a firefly, glowing with hope, with possibility. "Evie won't be there. She's still at school. You said so."

"There's only a week left of term. I've no work. And I can write to the school, or call even; tell Evie I'll be waiting, that I'll be there when she gets back. I need to get away." Her voice is softer now, kinder. "Not just from Penn. From all of it, all of this. Do you understand?"

He doesn't. Not at all. Because why go to Eden when this, right here, this is paradise.

"There's a train from Paddington tonight; a sleeper. I checked."

"When? When did you check?"

"You were asleep. I went to the phonebox."

"I could've come with you," he says. But it's desperate, and even he knows it.

"Look," she says, touching his arm, "I'll write. OK?"

He nods, defeated. And then quickly, efficiently, she is gone.

AUGUST 1988

"EVIE, PLEASE. You have to come."

Tom's at the window again, banging, calling my name. But something's changed. The anger is gone from his voice, and he sounds scared.

"What is it now?" I ask quickly, anxious for this to be over, so that Penn doesn't hear us or see us, and come down from his perch on the roof.

"Evie, Julia rang."

I feel a roll, like the lurch of a boat in a savage sea. But I knew this would happen. That she would try to put an end to it all.

"And what?" I ask, though I'm pretty sure I know the answer.

"She tried you but the line's dead."

"We unplugged it."

"Why?"

"So no one can tell us to stop. That's what she wants to do, isn't it? Tell me to grow up, to open the gates, to let the decorators in."

"Yes— no, I… Look. He's not who you think."

"What, you're jealous?" I say.

"Jesus, Evie. This is serious. What's his name?"

His name? "Penn," I say. "Will Pennington."

"He told you that, did he?"

"Yes. Of course. I'm—" sure he did? Am I? Or did I tell *him*? I think back, search my memory for that day, try to rerun the conversation, what I said, what he said.

"Will Pennington's still in Hampshire. Julia got a letter yesterday, asking to meet up with her in London."

I feel my legs begin to buckle and I grab the window sill to hold myself up.

"I don't believe you," I say. But maybe I do. Surely I do.

"Believe her, then. She's coming down tonight."

I feel my legs tremble again. Stand up! I scream at myself, be strong, be brave.

"Look, I don't think you should stay here. I don't know who that, that— man is, but he's not this Penn person."

I look up at the roof. And I see him there, leaning on the stone, watching us, listening to us.

"Go away," I say slowly, deliberately. Then, louder, desperate, "Leave me alone. Leave *us* alone." I slam the door, turn the lock, and lean against its solidity, wait for him to go. To call Julia. Call the police.

Leave us alone, I repeat, silently. But then another thought creeps in: Who is "us" any more? If he isn't Penn up on the roof, then who is he?

The truth will be in his rucksack. That's where he keeps his worldly possessions, the ones he can't store inside himself, for he refuses to hang anything in wardrobes or fold it into drawers. As if he's expecting a flood, or a siege, or a great, raging fire.

I turn it upside down, tip out a tumble of paperbacks and socks and other jetsam: a pine cone, a stone with a hole, a piece of snakeskin from the woods. And money. The muddle of banknotes inside that Jiffy bag I saw that first day. Is this the clue? But Penn is well-off. Having cash doesn't make him not Penn. But then, why so much? Why all in used notes? Why not a platinum credit card on Daddy's account?

But it's not enough evidence. I need something more. I root through the pile of stuff again, looking for rubies, for jewels, all the while hoping to get nothing but soil. And there it is – a gleaming Castafiore diamond, a Fabergé egg of a thing: a letter.

I turn it over in my hands, feel the crackle of it. The handwriting is cramped, contained, not the extravagant hand of the letter on Bea's dresser. And I feel the first blow, shattering the skimmed surface of our existence.

Then another: the address on the front is for a town in the North, a place I recognize from jokes about flat caps and whippets and the grimness of it all. But the name I don't know: "Brigid Sturridge". Who is she? Is she his girlfriend? Is that why he and Bea argued? Maybe there are more girls. Maybe there are hundreds of me in houses just like this.

But there is no other house like this, I think, and I tear open the letter. I am the only me. And he is Penn. He will be Penn.

But he's not. And the third blow strikes. Because the name at the bottom of the letter has no W or P. It begins instead with a J. Like the name he signed the day we bound our lives to each other. But it's not Jimmy Dean, the name he claimed for himself.

It's James Gillespie.

Oh God. I reel back, drop the letter as if it is searing the truth onto my skin. Because James Gillespie isn't a stranger. He's not just some chancer who happened to find the boathouse that day, who needed a bed, who wanted a girl, who went along with my story because it suited him.

No, I've heard of James Gillespie before. And I know where.

The letters are stuck between the pages of a book. The one with flying children and little lost boys. The one with Neverland. She sent them last year, before Christmas, before she swore never to come back and I swore never to speak to her again. I read them angrily then, hating her for this new life, wanting her to ask about mine, to come back to mine. But I was the bit part I'd always been, an afterthought. So I thrust them where they have sat ever since; a disappointment, saying nothing I needed to know or wanted to hear. But now, now they contain everything I need. Because in them are Penn, his wonder, his perfection, the conviction that he is the one who will end it all, all the flitting and flirting and never-quite-enough of the boys who have gone before. But there is someone else too: James. A boy she has met on her course, whom she thinks is odd, special. He's from the North: Wigan. And he's talented, a chameleon. "You should see him, Evie," she says. "He can be anyone, anyone he wants."

And I hear it now. The slips in his accent, the short vowel in "bath" sometimes. That time he said "aye" but meant "yes".

Tom was right. He's not who he says he is. And I should run. I should go now, flee into the woods and across the water to the village where I can sound the alarm.

But I need to know why. I need to ask him why he's done this thing to me. This terrible thing. And so I do run. But not down. I run along the corridor, and to the steps that lead to the attic, and beyond that, the roof. And with each step I feel the walls around me shatter, great yawning chasms ripping through the paint and paper, feel the flags crumble beneath my feet into powder and dust.

For the world has shifted on its axis: summer has turned to darkest winter; heaven to a seething, searing hell; and Eden, Eden is falling.

JULY 1988

PENN SITS *in a chair next to the bed; the hard wooden back forcing him out of his slouch into an uncomfortable upright position, and uncomfortable thoughts. For, as his father lies sallow and breath-laboured before him, patiently awaiting the cloaked death, the winged angels, all he can think about is Bea. Now she's gone he sees his life for what it is alone: shallow and colourless.*

He knows he's made a mistake. That Bea hasn't flown from him but that he pushed her, as he pushed the others. And he knows that he needs to get her back before it's too late.

That night he calls Hetty, who tells him Bea left three days ago. But when he phones the house on the hill, it's not her voice that answers but Hunter's.

"No idea, mate," he drawls when Penn demands to know where she is, where she's gone. "Not seen her in ages. Maybe she went home? In fact you're lucky you got me, going myself any minute."

Yes, thinks Penn, when he's hung up. She must have gone home. Gone back to Eden.

He calls the number she gave him last Christmas, recalls their conversation, drunk on advocaat and desperate to see each other, remembers her promise to come back the next day – a promise kept. He hears the echo of the bell at the other end of the line, imagines it ringing in a hallway that mirrors the one he stands in, calling her down a tiled corridor to him.

But this time she doesn't come. The phone rings into nothingness and he eventually hangs up.

She's on her way, he thinks then, his belief still burning strong, lighting his thoughts, lightening them. She's on a train, so he'll write and it'll get there tomorrow and she'll open it and realize he loves her and only her.

And then, when his father has gone, when he's free of this tomb of a house, he'll go to her, and begin life again.

The blind has been raised now, and James sits at the window. It's started to rain; fat drops falling fast from a black sky. He watches a drunk stagger under the streetlamps, a bus sending puddles sloshing from the gutter over his feet.

He sees it all, all the dirt and the sadness and the sheer, relentless poverty. No gold glints on the streets outside, just

*wet pavement, and inside the mould-stained walls, the bro-
ken lampshade. Why would she stay here, anyway? She needs
more, deserves more.*

So does he.

*And then he hears the scrape of starch and sulphur on
sandpaper. It's a tiny sound, but sharp, clear above the muffled hum of London. A match has been struck inside him.
He feels the prick of heat from the burst of phosphorous, and
then the answer to his problems is lit in front of him. White
words hang in the air, burnt on his retina long after the letters
have faded.*

*He will bring her back. Back to him, and only to him.
He'll be Robin Hood; he will steal from the rich. He knows
where to get money, and who to get it from. Then he can
buy her a life fit for a princess; for his Maid Marian. A life
so fabulous, and he so heroic, so special, that she will never
want to leave again.*

AUGUST 1988

I AM sick with dread, fear hardened into stone in my stomach as I climb out onto the bright, wide expanse of the roof. He's there, king of the world, watching the woods, the river, the sea. But I can't bear to look at it. Can hardly bear to look at him.

"Who are you?" I say.

"You know who I am."

"I know you're not Penn."

He stiffens but says nothing.

"I know your name is James Gillespie. Bea knew you. But I don't know who you were to her. Or who she was to you."

But still he won't answer me. And I'm angry now. I want

to hurt him like he has hurt me. "Did she laugh at you like she laughed at the others? Did she kiss you then run away? Yes, that's it. You wanted her, but you couldn't have her. So you thought you'd have me. So tell me, who are you?"

He turns now, his face contorted, his eyes alight, burning into me. "I'm Icarus," he booms, his voice deep, sonorous. "I'm Hamlet. I'm Superman. I'm Peter Fucking Pan. I'm untouchable. Can you feel it, Evie? Can you? Can you feel it in me?" He grabs one of my hands and presses it to his chest. I try to snatch it away but he grips harder, pulls me towards the edge. "Shall we fly, Evie? We could jump together. It would be perfect. The perfect end, do you see?"

"Don't be stupid," I manage to gasp.

"But I'm not. This is the most sensible thing we could do. The only thing we can do now. You and me against the world." His hand is bruising me now, forming a welt across my wrist.

"Please," I beg. "Let me go."

He turns to me and smiles. "I'll never let you go, Evie. Not you or Eden. You know that. You wanted this, remember. This was your idea."

And he is not lying now. He will not let me go. Not unless—

"OK," I say.

"Really?"

"Yes, I'll do it." I force a smile. Then I lift my head, lift my lips to his.

And it works. He drops my wrist to cup my face, to pull

222

me closer, but in that split second I curl my hand into a fist, and punch him hard in the stomach the way Bea taught me. He doubles up, coughing. I think he's going to vomit and for a second I worry that I've really hurt him. Then he looks up at me, eyes black with hate, and I run, faster than I have ever run before, my feet pounding the felting. I drop through the hatch, not caring that I'm going to fall to the floor. I stumble, and my knee scrapes the rough boards. It begins to bleed, but I don't have time to staunch it now. I can hear him following me.

"Evie!" he screams. "Come here."

But I'm gone, along the landing, into Aunt Julia's room. There's a phone in there. A spare one so she could have privacy to shout at Uncle John, to moan about the weather or the locals. I'll call the police, I think. And they will come, sirens screaming, and arrest him.

But when I get there the phone has gone. He must have hidden it when I slept. I feel a pain in my bladder, threatening to give way, my stomach rise in a cloud of butterflies. Not now, I plead. I have to hide. I have to hide.

I'm hidden. Pushed to the back of the cupboard in the coats and the cloaks and the fur. I hear his footsteps creak along the boards, for he doesn't know their secrets, not like Bea and I. "I know you're in there," he calls. "I'm coming to get you." He's angry now. Doors are flung open and then kicked shut again. Curtains are pulled from their poles, the rings clattering to the floor. Then there are more footsteps, and something moves on the other side of the door, blocking the light from the keyhole momentarily. He's there. He has found me. I can hear his breath, heavy and fast. Just as he must be able to hear mine. I wait for the handle to turn. Wait for him to say "Got you."

But instead I hear a retreat. His rasping breath fades with his footsteps down the corridor. It's a trick, I think. He's crept back silently and is waiting behind the door to pounce on me when I open it.

But then I hear the tread of feet on gravel outside, then the clank of a heavy iron latch being lifted and dropped. The outhouse. He thinks I am in the outhouse.

It's my last chance. I have to get out of Eden and into the woods before he realizes his mistake. He won't remember the way, I think; he only came here once and in the dim light of the storm. And so I run. No, I fly – fly between oaks and ashes, through deep puddles that shower my legs with filth. I am halfway there now, can see the tin roof of the boathouse through the trees – a beacon, a buoy.

But then I catch sight of something else. A flash of a figure in red to the side of me. What was he wearing? Oh shit, it's him. It has to be him. I don't have to time to get *Jorion*. Think. Think… I will swim across the creek. I'm faster and stronger than him in the water. I swerve to take the short cut around the boathouse. But as I reach the edge of the makeshift quay, my flip-flop catches on something, and I feel myself falling; can almost see myself fast and slow all at once, tumbling through air, as the viscous green of the water comes up to meet me. I hit my head on the hard, grey stone beside the creek.

Then all I see is black.

JULY 1988

BEA SITS on the bed in the attic at Telegraph Hill, her arms gripped tightly around cold, bare legs, her world up-ended. She sees now what love can do, what havoc it can wreak, what lives it can destroy. But she'll make it all right; with Evie and Tom, with her mother and father even. She'll go back to Eden and open the house, decorate it, throw a welcome party like no other, have a last summer to end all summers before the house is sold and they must all move on to new lives.

She checks her watch and realizes she has been sat here too long. The vodka – her Dutch courage – has length-ened the seconds into minutes, minutes into hours. It's ten now and she can't reach Paddington in time to catch the train, not even in a taxi. But there's no urgency, not really. She'll just go in the morning. She'll feel better then anyway, after she's slept and taken a shower; washed the smell of him from her.

It's one in the morning. The rain has stopped now and the air on Telegraph Hill is clearer, cooler than the exhaust-wrapped smog of the Old Kent Road. But James is hot. He is on fire.

The plan is simple. And he is a fucking genius. He is Superman; he is the Wonderful Wizard of Oz; he is Batman and the Joker, Sherlock and Moriarty all at once.

The windows of Penn's house are black, dead eyes to the world. No one is home, just like she said. He slips his hand under the mat. WELCOME, it says, and he replies with a silent thank you as he feels the cold, hard outline of a single key.

He lets himself in, then listens. But the house says nothing, and he hears only the electric hum of the fridge. He'll be quick anyway, just in case someone comes back.

Penn keeps it in a tin under his bed; Bea told him. Dirty money stashed away from the Coutts account – and the eyes of his father – to pay for the next eight-bar, the next ounce, the next obliterated night.

James sits down on the floor, legs crossed, the tin in his lap. Then he lifts the lid, opening it slowly, carefully, like it is a chest of buried treasure.

And it is treasure.

Ten, twenty, a hundred, a thousand. I'm Robin Hood, he repeats to himself as he sets the notes in piles. I'm stealing from the rich, and the lazy and the stupid, to give to the poor. I'm a hero, he thinks, and the thought is edifying.

There's nearly two thousand in there. Enough for him to make a start somewhere bigger, better than his flat on the Old Kent Road. He'll get an apartment in Docklands maybe, high up in a tower, where everything is shiny and new. No cracks and stains and reminders of what used to be. He stuffs the money in a Jiffy envelope he finds on the desk. Then next to it he sees a packet of Marlboro. Penn's cigarettes; Jimmy Dean's cigarettes – not like the roll-ups he has to smoke. He'll have one, he decides. He deserves one. And so he takes the Zippo and runs his thumb sharply on the flint, and a petrol-blue flame flickers and fills the room with a dull glow.

But, as he lifts it towards the cigarette in his mouth he has a sobering, sinking thought. What if Penn begs her to come back to him? What if he promises her riches: clothes, jewels, his undying, unwavering love? Promises to marry her. Promises her the house, this house. That they can be there together, just the two of them.

And it comes to him in another match-bright burst. He has to destroy what Penn has. He has to burn it, just like his dad did. Burn it all: the swirling Van Gogh whirls of orange-starred carpet; the bed where he fucked her, betrayed her; the blue-faced lady looking down on it all. Then, out of the ashes they will rise, he and Bea, into a new, light, bright day; fly to the sun-skimming tower in the East. Because then she cannot go back, can never go back.

And so he lights up the cigarette, but instead of taking a long, low drag, he pushes the red tip slowly, carefully into the cotton of the bedspread; waits for smoke to curl, sending white tendrils to the ceiling; waits for the small brown hole to spread, to eat up the fabric, its edges hot, hungry. The voices in his head begin to speak. *This is it,* they say. *You've done it. You've won.* They clamour, proclaiming his triumph, applauding his heroism. And they're loud, so loud now that they drown out the fridge, and the crackle of the flames that lick at the wallpaper, and his own footsteps retreating down the tiled hallway.

And they're loud enough to drown out the sound of a girl far up and away in the attic, as she turns heavily in her drink-soaked sleep, a packed rucksack next to her bed, and thoughts of Eden dancing in her dreams.

AUGUST 1988

WHEN I come to, the first sensation is one of pain; a deep throbbing in my forehead, the sharp sting of cuts across my calves and thighs wet with salt water. I'm dizzy, too, so that when I try to stand, a whirl of shooting stars dances in front of my eyes, a giddy merry-go-round, a Catherine wheel set off inside my head.

"Don't," he says. "Don't try to move. Not yet."

I start at the voice.

"It's OK, Evie. It's all OK now."

"Tom."

As if by magic, he came. He came and pulled me from the water.

I'm safe, I think. Nothing else can happen now. Nothing

can harm me. I should never have doubted it – doubted him.

And yet, something is wrong. Something… What is it? I turn this way and that, searching for the missing piece. Then I catch it again, on the wind.

Smoke. Something's burning. But it's not the fields this time, not the stubble of wheat and corn. It's an acrid, tainted, smell: rubber and plastic and the nylon of new carpet; and older things too – wood panels, velvet drapes, the foxed pages of books.

Eden. Eden is on fire.

"The h–house." I find my voice, a scratchy stammer at first, then a painful, screaming sound, a keening. "The house!" I haul myself to my feet.

"Don't," Tom begs. "You can't."

But I have to, because that house is all I have of Bea. She's in there, somewhere. And I can't let this happen again.

"I'm coming with you then," he says, and he puts one arm around my waist, then holds me as we drag and stumble our way back to Eden.

I don't know what I hoped for or expected. Did I want James to be inside, his body blackened on a funeral pyre of fur coats and beaded dresses? Or did I pray that, having quenched the fire to a plume of smoke with buckets of water, he had collapsed on the lawns, sobbing?

But the scene that confronts us is neither of these. In this picture, he's standing on the sweep of gravel in front of the house: tall, magnificent, his eyes alight with reflected flames, his limbs burning with his own internal electricity.

"James," Tom says, carefully, so as not to startle him. "James, what have you done?"

He doesn't turn, but carries on staring, crazed, into the ravenous fire that chews through Eden's curtains with its charred teeth and dragon's breath. "Do you see it, Evie?" he says. "Do you? No one can take Eden now. It's yours for ever. This is for you. I did it all for you. Just like I did for Bea, too. I burned Telegraph Hill so that she'd be free. Free from him. From that – that fake, that charlatan. Then she could be with me. But she – she—"

It takes a second for what he's saying to sink in. And then it all falls into place. Images flash across my inward eye: Bea asleep in the house on Telegraph Hill. *CLICK*. James letting himself in. *CLICK*. Him watching flames take hold, feeling the power in his hands, to destroy, to create. *CLICK*.

I let out a sound, an animal sound, a half moan. "You killed her. You killed Bea."

"She shouldn't have been there," he spits, like it's her fault. "She should have been on the train. She said she was catching the train."

"But she didn't," I sob. "She stayed." He didn't burn her past. He burned her now, her future, all our futures.

I look at him. At this man, this boy, this pathetic, never-grown-up Peter Pan, standing wide-eyed and desperate. I hate him. I should hit him, launch myself at his body, my fists pummelling into his chest, his stomach, his face. Should avenge Bea, should avenge myself, for it is me he is burning now, me he is destroying. But the fight is gone.

In the distance I hear the sound of sirens, then the angry buzzing of a saw or cutters, of blades slicing through a padlock. Not even iron can keep the world out. We were never safe. We were fools. I was a fool.

I hear movement behind me, feel a hand rest on my shoulder.

"We'll take it from here, son."

A man in uniform, a policeman or ambulance driver maybe, lifts my arm, detaching me from Tom. He pulls to resist.

"It's OK, you can come," the man says. "We'll need to check both of you."

"What about him?" I say, pointing at James. "What will happen to him?"

"We'll check him too. But the police want to see him."

Something flaps past me on the wind. A singed paper, or a moth, shaken from its sleep by the heat and noise. I gasp.

"Come on, love."

The man lifts me, so that I'm suspended between him and Tom, my legs useless, dangling, the toes barely touching the ground. They turn me towards the ambulance, but when I strain my head to find the moth, the mote, again. But when I look, it's gone, and in its place I see her. I see Bea. But she isn't scared, she isn't screaming. She is still, calm. For now it's over. Now I know. Now she can leave. We can both leave.

JULY 1988

JAMES WAKES *late, turns over in his bed and hears a crackle, feels a strange lump under him, digging into the small of his back. He reaches down and pulls out a fat brown envelope, and then he smiles. He did it. He is Dick Whittington after all. He is Superman. He is a Knight in Shining Armour. Wait till I tell Bea, he thinks; till she comes back and sees what I've found, what I've stolen for her.*

It's four days before James knows the truth of what he's done.

He's sitting in a café, a cracked mug of tea and a copy of Loot *on the Formica in front of him. The page is marked; inky rings of hope circling flats in Chelsea, Clapham, Canary Wharf. Places with ambition, like him.*

A workman in site-blackened boots and the bright orange of a high-vis jacket rises from a table across the aisle. He carries a copy of the South London Press *in his hand.*

"Want this, son?" he offers.

James doesn't usually read the papers. They're too full of sad lives and half achievements. But he's got nothing else to do until his first viewing in Docklands at four, then ten long weeks stretching out in front of him until she comes back. And this will fill an hour.

"Cheers," he says. And turns to the front page.

NOW

EDEN WAS alight for two days while men battled to save her. But she was too far gone; James had done too good a job. By the time the engines got there the flames had taken hold of the attic, smoke billowing from windows blackened like poked-out eyes. And the sound; God, the sound. No one tells you what fire sounds like. It's not the gentle crackle of logs behind a grate, but a great, creaking, sucking, deafening roar, a thundering noise of death, destruction. Did Bea hear this? I thought. Did she wake, screaming, to the splintering of floorboards, the crash of lintels falling through floors? But I have to let the thoughts go, let them fly on the wind like charred slips of paper, of curtain, of letters once squirrelled away; ephemera now.

I can't let myself be her. I can't remember the way she died, only the way she lived – burning bright and soaring above us all.

"If you play with fire, you get burned." I remember Aunt Julia's words; a warning to me and Bea as we sat on the scullery floor striking matches in turn. But still we played a dangerous game.

Now, each time I'm pulled back from my dreams of Eden, to the now-me, I begin another, a game of "what ifs" and "if onlys".

What if I'd replied to Bea's letters, instead of sinking into a sullen, stubborn silence; my fragile, egotistical self still smarting from the fact that she had another life about which to write at all?

What if I'd done as Aunt Julia asked – begged – and left in June, gone with her to her new apartment and new life in London?

What if I'd listened to Tom that time, instead of dismissing his pleas, his protestations about Penn as nothing more than the powder-light residue of his vague affection for me, or for Bea?

Would it have been different if I'd been different? If I'd been stronger? Taller? If my hair had been cropped or curled, or shone with the brilliance of bottle blonde, instead of falling in dark, heavy hanks? If I'd been more like her? Or nothing like her at all?

What if it had happened today, now that we have Google

and Facebook, now that our lives trail through the ether like a stick dragged in sand; names and faces and deeds trapped like flies in the invisible amber of the internet?

If I could turn back time, if I could alter just one of these, would Bea be alive, filling my head, my heart, with her wild ideas, her unfailing conviction? Would Eden still stand, a jewel, its dull glint flickering in the dark hand of the forest?

But then I put away the dice, the cards. Because I can't change what has been; only what I take from it.

I went to see him once in prison, years later. He'd written a letter, asked if I would come. When I saw it on our hall-way floor, when I recognized that handwriting spelling out my maiden name in spidery biro, I felt my stomach surge, smelled matches in the air. It took me a week to open the envelope, still longer to agree to go. But go I did. I had to. I had to hear what he had to say.

Sorry. That was it. He wanted to say sorry. For Bea, and for Eden. He'd meant to say it when he came to Cornwall. He'd thought if I was like Bea, then I might understand why he'd done it, that I might understand him. Then, when I thought he was Penn, he'd let me believe it. I asked him why, but he didn't know, other than jealousy and a talent for pretending.

He was someone else, he told me, when he did it, when he set the fires. Not himself; not James or even Seamus. He said he'd been diagnosed with some kind of disorder. I forget the name. But it meant he lost pockets of time, time when he turned himself into a greater version of himself, a superhero almost. Or a villain.

Penn doesn't understand why I went to see him. Said he could have killed me. Like he killed her. For of course I met Penn, the real Penn. We take tea sometimes, in the staid, sleek-carpeted lounge of a hotel in Piccadilly. Though less frequently these days, for work and children take up his time, as they do mine.

But what Penn cannot see, cannot admit, is that I was dead already, a corpse trapped in that coffin of a house, of a life. I thought I wanted Eden. I thought Eden was my freedom. But instead it had become my prison.

Maybe James knew that. Maybe he blew away my past like ashes on the salt wind. And, like a phoenix – like the bird he'd had tattooed on his shoulder in a Manchester back street – I rose, stronger, more alive. Maybe.

And without me and James, there would be no me and Tom.

Yes, Tom. It didn't start at once. I didn't stay with him at the Millhouse, I went to Aunt Julia's first, and then school; a new one, a day school. It was seven years later; I'd finished my Masters and was sitting in a café in Paris, in the 6th, reading a paperback in the first of the spring sunshine. And when I looked up, there he was. As if by magic.

Bea was right. There is a wide, wonderful world out there. A giant Eden.

And every day I am thankful to walk in it.

JOANNA NADIN has been thrice nominated for the title Queen of Teen for her bestselling Rachel Riley series. She is also the author of many award-winning books for younger children, as well as two compelling teen novels for Walker, *Wonderland* and *Undertow*. A former special adviser to the prime minister, she also freelances as a government speechwriter. She lives in Bath with her daughter, Millie.

About writing *Eden*, Joanna says: "*Eden* is about how place and people create us, and whether we can or should try to escape and lead other lives, even ones that don't at first appear to be our own. But above all, it's a love story; love for a house, a river, a boy, and a girl who shone brighter than I."